Praise for *Grace Notes*

'Heart and soul triumph over Covid lock~~down restrict~~ions in Karen Comer's debut verse novel. Art and music both soar, tremble, then take steadfast hold of the lives of Grace and Crux as they chart restrictions at home, in friendships and in lockdowns. Karen has used the verse novel to beguile, dance and demand layers of emotion and depth that only poetry can sustain. A masterful debut!'

Lorraine Marwood, author of *Footprints on the Moon* and *Leave Taking*

'Like the grace note of the title, this beautiful story strikes the perfect tone – mixing colour, light and music at a time when we needed it most.'

Nicole Hayes, author of *One True Thing* and *A Shadow's Breath*

'Poetry, music and art, woven together in an uplifting story about endless lockdowns and first love . . . Just wonderful.'

Nova Weetman, author of *The Jammer* and *Sick Bay*

'Karen Comer in *Grace Notes* has written something truly extraordinary. An honest and bruising mapping of Melbourne's pandemic year, that transcends and uplifts in verse form – like a symphonic crescendo – into an examination and rumination on the power of art. The creative outlet of two teenagers is beautifully celebrated here, as they persevere and hope through a gruelling year; daring to create and share their art, to let light in, and just connect – with themselves, each other, a ghost city, and a stopped world. A classic in the making; *Grace Notes* is a vital balm of a book, a story to press into everybody's hands.'

Danielle Binks, author of *The Year the Maps Changed* and *The Monster of Her Age*

GRACE NOTES

KAREN COMER

LOTHIAN

for Brett,
Tom, Annalise and Joe,
who shared
all six of Melbourne's lockdowns with me –
together we experienced all 52 shades of the cyanometer

Quote on page v from Banksy, *Wall and Piece*, Century, London, 2005, reproduced with permission

hachette
AUSTRALIA

Published in Australia and New Zealand in 2023
by Hachette Australia
(an imprint of Hachette Australia Pty Limited)
Gadigal Country, Level 17, 207 Kent Street, Sydney, NSW 2000
www.hachette.com.au

Hachette Australia acknowledges and pays our respects to the past, present and future Traditional Owners and Custodians of Country throughout Australia and recognises the continuation of cultural, spiritual and educational practices of Aboriginal and Torres Strait Islander peoples. Our head office is located on the lands of the Gadigal people of the Eora Nation.

A catalogue record for this book is available from the National Library of Australia

ISBN: 978 0 7344 2172 2 (paperback)

Cover design and additional internal typography by Astred Hicks, Design Cherry
Cover and internal art by Karen Farmer (@karen_farmer)
Text design by Bookhouse, Sydney
Typeset in 11.2/13.9 pt Bembo by Bookhouse, Sydney
Printed and bound in Great Britain by Clays Ltd, Elcograf S.p.A.

MIX
Paper | Supporting
responsible forestry
FSC® C018072

I get most joy in life out of music.

Albert Einstein

Imagine a city where graffiti wasn't illegal, a city where everybody could draw whatever they liked. Where every street was awash with a million colours and little phrases. Where standing at a bus stop was never boring. A city that felt like a party where everyone was invited, not just the estate agents and barons of big business. Imagine a city like that and stop leaning against the wall — it's wet.

Banksy

CRUX

This wall by the Yarra River is overflowing
with art and opinions and tags
so thick, the loudness of
the images and words
threaten me
with their confidence
and I wonder whether there'll
    ever
        be space
                for me.

Colours, mixed up with
political messages, lettering at least
half a metre high, sharp stencil
lines alongside eggshell stickers of
swirly shapes, tags with no
refined technique, letters so
unrecognisable the names aren't
clear, pieces fading near the top of the wall where
the artists couldn't reach.

There's a guy,
baggy shorts, paint-stained shirt,
at the other end of the wall, pulling out
spray cans from a backpack.

I stand by my skateboard,
looking at him and his cans.

He sprays a few sharp black lines
in a diamond pattern on the wall,
then goes over it

with a silhouette of a man parachuting.
He reaches for a couple of bright-coloured cans.

It's the clinking sound of the marbles shaking
within the can, mixing up paint,
that edges me closer to him.

Hey,
your lines, how'd you get them so thin?
Even with a skinny cap?

He stops shaking his can, grins.
Thanks, mate, he says.
You gotta get up close to the wall,
almost scrape the can against it.
You paint?

Yeah, nah, kinda.
My contradictory words are entirely true.

Yeah,
I paint.
I paint with cans
on cardboard, canvas,
the walls of our garage.

Nah,
I'm not
even legally
allowed to buy cans
until I reach eighteen.

Kinda,
Dad buys
spray cans for me,
I've painted the garage
twenty-three times in five years.

Just at home, I tell him.

Mate, you're missing the thrill.
He holds out his hand.
I'm Mack.

Crux. I shake his hand.
Wait, you're Mack?

I saw his latest on Instagram –
overscale dark figures,
diamond-bright background,
all angles and sharp geometric lines.
Made me feel confused,
like I was in the dark with his characters,
unaware of the brilliance behind them.

That's me.

He grabs a can,
tests the thickness of the paint
on the ground,
fills in a few diamond shapes with orange. The can
is covered with smears of paint,
expertise and creativity.
Then he sprays yellow;
the donut on the top of the can
– the ring of colour around the nozzle –
is a murky yellow
beneath the splotches of other colours.

He nods at my phone
sticking out of my pocket.
Show me your stuff,
before I do the next layer.

Your owl's good.
Great feathers, lots of movement.
But the eyes, they need more depth.
See, like Bindy's.
He points to the wall,
to a realistic koala clinging to a tree
in front of a raging inferno.

You know Bindy?
I'm doing my goldfish gaping mouth –
my sister Molly's description.
Quick snap shut.

Yeah,
done some work together.
Abbotsford, Fitzroy, the city.
Bindy's work is realistic.
But I like to add something different to my eyes.
See? He shows me on his phone.
There's an old man with oversized eyes,
and within the eyes is a reflection.
But it's an internal reflection,
a tiny picture of a younger man dancing.

Mind. Blown.

Mack uses green
to sign his name,
finish his piece.

Done.
Hey, shoot me a message later?
I'll let you know when we're meeting next.
Bindy, Uni-girl, Fendix . . .
You can come,
I'll show you how to paint eyes.

Mack picks up his backpack,
flicks his hand goodbye,
walks away.

I'm in!
If I could paint
on this wall right now
I'd spray an arc of blue
so wide it could capture
all possibilities –

Sign my name.

—

Don't even have to change
my name for my art –
it already works.

I'm really James Michael Crux
but only Mum calls me that, sometimes.

I'm Crux,
Dad's called Cruxy.
I'm like Dad, everyone says –
creative hands, shaggy brown hair, tall.

You'd think with my name and height
I'd play a brilliant game of footy.
Centre half-forward or ruck
in the middle of the pack,
heart of the goal square.

Crux of the team.

I do play footy,
make the C team – just.

Ascend into the pack for a couple of marks,
kick the odd goal.

But usually,
I paint oversized birds,
spray-paint them into existence
on one side of Dad's garage.

Before I skate home,
I take my cyanometer out, hold it
up to the sky.
A solid 12 now.

I know it's weird
that I love
this acrylic ring so much.
I know blueness can't really be measured,
that no-one can really gauge the blueness of the sky.

But one scientist tried.
Horace Bénédict de Saussure created a paper circle
painted with fifty-two grades of blue –
a cyanometer.
You hold it up to the sky and
with your eye
find the closest match.

There's a cyanometer app,
but I prefer this model
Dad gave me four years ago.

I wrap my cyanometer back in its soft pouch,
skate home through
the solid blueness

of Mack's invite,
as if the sky had wrapped
all its possibilities around me.

Grace

Ettie's tram glows yellow and green,
sturdy among the late summer leafiness
in the park opposite her nursing home.

Her tram is always available,
open,
ready for anyone to come in,
sit, think, play a while
in this stationary tram
that once trundled along city tracks.

I slide into a curved wooden seat,
touch the oak leaves from a branch
that has grown through the glassless window,
flick a few cigarette butts into the corner with my foot
and check Rani's text again.

> I'm singing in Jay's bar,
> need a violinist.
> Thursdays, 5.30–7.
> Interested?
> This would be so good for you, Grace!

I know Jay's bar.
Been there a few times with Rani,
sitting in front of the stage, watching
her and her muso friends perform.
Jay runs around,

organises the events,
plays the piano.
My real-life thumb hovers over
the thumbs-up icon.
Maybe together the physical and virtual thumbs
are strong enough to overcome
Mum's inevitable objection.

Probably not.
I turn my phone off.

I leave Ettie's tram,
cross the road
to her aged care home.

The welcome sign, ever cheerful,
shows no signs
of the despair that seeps
from under the front door.

There's a little posse of residents
clustered in the foyer.
Helena reaches out to touch my cheek.
Creepy the first time she did it
but now I lean in toward her.

Dad told me once
that these faded women,
with their corrugated skin and trembling limbs,
wait at the front door for the children
around 3.30 every afternoon.

Whose children? I asked.

Their children.
Their internal clock

tells them
when it's time for the kids
to come home from school.

Sometimes, Helena's waiting
for her little boy, now an adult son, to visit.
She is so beautifully heartbreaking I can't bear it,
like a high note on the E string
played after a long
pause.

———

Ettie's in her room, sitting
in her favourite floral-covered armchair,
the one she brought from home,
reading her book.

She could be the poster girl
for the nursing home –
See how content she looks!

Darling!
she calls, all elegance as she airily waves an arm
in my direction.

I lean over, kiss her red-capillaried cheek,
breathe in Ettieness.
'Essence of Ettie', my family calls it.

I take out my violin,
rub rosin along the hair of the bow,
open up the tuning app on my phone.

Another graceful arm movement from Ettie,
her right arm only.

Put that thing away.
She mocks me with a smile.
I'll tell you.

I run my bow along each string,
listen to the open chord, to Ettie's direction,
then adjust the fine tuners
with micro movements,
until her sensitive ear and my violin are aligned.

Now, play for me.

The Verve would never have envisioned
their 'Bitter Sweet Symphony'
played in a nursing home
by a granddaughter for her Ettie,
who taps the beat on her book with her one good hand.

I'd usually play for an hour,
with Ettie correcting my bowing –
    gently, gently –
or reminding me of my intonation –
    softly, softly.

But she seems tired today, even though
she looks at me
as if I am the most important thing in the world.

I hug her frail self goodbye,
promise to visit again next week,
leave early.

—

When I was little-little –
pumpkin on my face,

afternoon nap little –
I used to twirl, dance, sing my way
to the park, the library,
to bath, to bed.

My older sisters Liv and Sam
would sometimes follow me,
sometimes shush me.
And I would sing a little louder.

But when Dad showed me
Ettie's violin
resting in its case,
I was silent.

I plucked a string
with a gentle finger.
The tone filled the kitchen,
filled me.

I didn't choose to play the violin.
The violin chose me.
Not Liv, not Sam.
Me.

Corona chorus

Wednesday, 26 February 2020
Daily Victoria Covid statistics
New cases: 0
Total cases: 1
Deaths: 0

JacksonzB71
This'll be over soon –
Covid is just a bad cold.

OrganicBathtubs
Hope they're screening
international travellers.

Grumpy_Goose
Feeling worried –
cases already in Aus.

CRUX

School finished, sports training done,
I walk in through the side door.
The usual scene at home – the beginnings
of dinner on the kitchen bench,
a pot plant trailing its spidery leaves
over a newspaper,
an oil burner sending out wafts of geranium,
a book open on the table,
Mum's bizarre three-headed goddess sculpture-thing,
– baring EVERYTHING –
on a kitchen shelf.

Wash your hands, says Mum automatically,
glancing up from the couch and TV.

I rinse my hands in the kitchen sink,
half-watch the news.

The report flashes to hospital scenes
in China. There are people
in masks buying food,
lining hospital corridors,
waiting outside clinics
to be tested for this virus –
coronavirus.
Covid-19.
Then there are scenes from Italy –
it's chaotic,
people look frightened.

It's really contagious, Mum says, frowning.
Already a few cases in Australia.
Her fingers stroke the purple stone in her hand.

Stop being a nurse at home, I tease.
You don't have to care for these people –
they're not your patients.
I flop down next to her on the couch.

Mum picks up my hand,
inspects it for cleanliness.

I pull it away,
mock-roll my eyes at her.
I'm fifteen! Stop mothering! Stop nursing!

She gives me her look –
closed-up mouth but bright eyes.
Not so easy to stop either.
She stretches an arm around me,
and I let her pull me in,
even though I'm bigger than her.

Molly runs down the stairs,
plonks herself down on the couch next to me.
Loser, she says affectionately,
twisting the neck of my black t-shirt.

Idiot, I return with equally friendly feeling.

Aren't you two old enough
to stop this now? Mum asks.

Never! we say in tandem.

—

Dad's given me a quarter of the garage.
Pretty generous
considering there's a car,
Christmas decorations,

boxes labelled 'stuff'
and Dad's gadgets. And his equipment.
Tools and leather.
He makes leather kits as a side hustle –
wallets, bags, pouches, key rings.
It balances out his job as a camera operator
for a Melbourne news team.

My quarter
has an old easel splattered in paint, dozens
of canvases stacked against
the wall – covered with
a powerful owl, wings extended
fully – plus three milk crates full
of spray cans.

Dad's already working in there,
car parked in the driveway, 90s music
in the background.
I've learned a lot of lyrics from the 90s.

He nods at me, pauses
punching holes into leather pieces.
How was your day?

Alright. Yours?

Busy. Lots of talk about this coronavirus.

I haven't talked to Dad about Mack.
Half of me wants to tell him –
I met a street artist!
The other half knows
if Dad even suspects I'd go out painting
he'd stop buying cans.

We made an agreement –
he'd buy the cans with the money
I earn from my supermarket job
if I promised not to paint in the streets
until I finished school.

Education first,
don't
get into trouble,
then you can do what you want, he'd said.

Dad's in this brother-to-brother program –
Nathan Crux, mentor.
He spends time with kids who have
    parents who are drug-addicted,
    alcoholic,
    violent,
    or have a mental illness,
        or maybe the kids are drug addicts themselves,
        alcoholic,
        violent,
        or have their own mental illness.

He wants to protect Molly and me.
Wrap us in cotton wool, Molly says.
Keep you straight, Dad says.

I pull out my iPad, open up Procreate,
start a new piece –
draw a masked doctor in scrubs
with a huge line of patients in front of him.
No colour yet,
just sketching the outline.

But I can't quite get it right –
stuffed up the perspective.

Dad tidies up his tools,
comes over to see my work
but doesn't comment.
He pats my shoulder
with leather-smelling hands.
Have a break, dinner's ready.

Grace

My violin teacher, Rani,
has known me since forever.

As soon as I arrive at her house,
there's a patter of running, jumping footsteps,
and her two small boys open the door to me.

Grace! they shout,
hurl themselves around my legs.

I high-five them. *Hey, guys!*

Rani untangles them.
Grace is here for her lesson,
which is just about the length of your movie.

Her voice is mum-in-charge, don't mess with me, kids,
but her smile shows
her mother-heart,
full of nursery rhymes and sticky hugs.
Heartbeat quick,
    semi-quaver quick
      lucky kids
        to have her heartbeat
          metronome steady.

She points the control at the TV
with the precision of a conductor,
and leads me to her studio.
Warm up with your scales, she says,
lowering a music stand for me.
Legato, then detaché.

My violin always feels warm,
like there's still a breath in it
from the spruce tree,
from the maple tree,
living wood
cut down, carved out
to create a stringed voice.
There's still a life-force that sings
and can't ever be suppressed,
even when my violin lies alone in its case.

What do you think about my gig? Rani asks.
Paying job, and it'd be great experience for you.

My bow glides over the strings,
the chords perfectly pitched.

She slides onto the piano seat.
You're ready.
None of this school concert stuff anymore.

She's hit a dissonant nerve –
I'm so tired of playing the same pieces
over and over in orchestra,
waiting for everyone to catch up,
no room for expression,
no space for me.

I want you to improvise,
read the mood, follow my cues,
anticipate what the pianist will do.
What do you think?
Let me know if you want me to persuade
your mum.

Ha! She might take
some persuading, I say.
She's away — I'll have to message her.

Rani angles her head to the side,
the way she always does
when she wants me to think through
a challenging piece.

Your mum wants the best for you.
You just disagree on exactly
what that is.

——

After my lesson,
I meander home
through Richmond's streets,
both narrow and wide,
with skinny, single-fronted houses
and towering apartment blocks.
Rani's jazz violin
fills my head and heart,
while I think about playing in Jay's bar.

Equal parts hope and hopelessness.

I unlock the front door
of our weatherboard house,

soft grey boards, charcoal grey trim.
Wait for Griffin,
our tangle-haired teddy of a dog,
to meet me as usual.
No-one else home.

Hey hey, Griffin,
how was your day?
Bet it was peaceful,
bet you didn't have to make
any big decisions,
I say, scratching him
on top of his head.

I'm about to open the fridge
but I pause to re-read the notes there
from Mum, even though
they've been up for a week.

> Liv,
>> cancel your bakery shifts for next week –
>> you have too much study to do.
>
> Sam,
>> good luck for your netball trials
>> but don't forget to study for the next
>> French test.
>
> Grace,
>> remember to do an extra maths question
>> every night. Maths first, violin second.
>
> See you soon,
> Love, Mum XXX

It still feels unusual for Mum to be away
in Italy. Away from us,
away from her job as a lawyer in a city firm.

She's gone there for a few weeks
to shop and see the sights.
    In that order.

Mum is a big shopper –
she likes her things.
I turn and look around the kitchen
and family-room –
beautiful art on every wall,
too many cushions on the couch,
fancy sculptural ornaments on the shelves.

I don't want things, I want
POSSIBILITIES,
I say to Griffin.

Our conversation is interrupted
by Liv and Sam coming in the door,
late home after a VCE study session in the library –
Liv's in Year 12, Sam in Year 11.
There are benefits
to being the third daughter sometimes –
I get to see how Liv and Sam navigate life.

We shuffle around the kitchen bench,
getting snacks,
tripping over Griffin and schoolbags.
I can hear Mum's voice in my head:
Bags in the laundry, girls!
But she's not here to enforce it.

We are three in a row behind the bench
when Dad walks in the door,
home from work,

training communication leaders
to be nimble, flexible, agile.

My Lear daughters three! He smiles
and plants a kiss each
on our dark curly hair.

Ready art thou for netball practice? he asks Sam,
car keys still in his hand, misquoting Shakespeare.
Matt Dalfinch, comedian – not.

So glad it's Mum who's away,
not Dad.
Even if he thinks he's funny.
Even if he shares Mum's high standards.

———

If our family
had to be labelled in a word:
Over-
      achievers.

The Dalfinch family
      achieve and
      succeed and
      outperform and
      perfect and
      power through and
      make everyone around us
      shake their heads in admiration
      at our abilities.

We win awards,
    lead the team,
    play the solo,
    captain the side,
    address the board of directors,
    earn postnominals.

We are the Dalfinches,
    even Mum,
    even though she uses her maiden name.

And if we fail even slightly
in our brilliance –
there are two choices:

Work harder, then succeed.

OR

Don't. Even. Bother.

CRUX

Mack messages me with an address:

> Come over to the warehouse at 5.30.
> The others will be there.

—

The warehouse is down a lane
sprayed with art
by artists
whose work I worship.

There's music coming from the warehouse,
loud, on a Monday evening.

I tug at my favourite t-shirt —
small flecks of paint to show I'm serious,
not so much
that I look like I'm trying too hard.
          Although I am.

I knock on the door
— even the door is covered in art,
Kasper's trademark eyes and lines —
and roll back and forth on my feet.

No-one answers.

I knock louder.
The only way to get anywhere with street art
is to hang with other artists,
          paint with them,
          learn their techniques,
          earn their respect.
Every single street-art podcast, article, YouTube video
has told me this.

Keep knocking, I tell myself.

A man comes up behind me.
Hey! You going in?
Don't wait for them.

He wears a checked shirt, torn,
and a purple beanie,
carries a sixpack of beer,
looks like he's in his early twenties.
Fendix, he says, holding out his hand.

Crux,
voice rough.
Better too low than too high.

You're the kid who paints birds.
Mack told me.
Great YouTube videos, pro.
He grins,
opens the colourful, swirly door, waves me

through.

Gulp. He's watched my videos.
Fendix, painter of silos throughout Victoria –
awesome portraits of rural people –
has watched my videos.

Hey, says Fendix, striding in.
Found him outside.
His voice sounds kinder than his words.

Feet roll,
stop,
stop,
stop.

Mack jumps up from a couch
with the stuffing spilling out.

This here
is Crux.
You might have seen his birds on socials.

The only girl there, lolling
against a sprayed piano, smiles at me.
I know your birds!
Nice feathers.

I blush a thanks
at her summer-tan face,
bleached blonde hair.

I'm Issa,
but I paint as Uni-Girl.

You do all the chalk characters, right?

That's me!

She looks Molly's age,
maybe eighteen or nineteen.

Another guy in his twenties
comes forward,
smiles through his beard,
holds out his hand.
I'm Bindy,
welcome to the warehouse, mate.

I smile,
tell myself to relax.
I'm in, I'm here.

                              And Dad doesn't know.

The artists talk loudly around an old table,
        voices rising,
        banter flying,
        laughter vying
        for attention.

I'm trying to focus on them
but I sneak looks around the warehouse.

Mack offers me a beer,
and before I can think of what to say, like:
    – I'm fifteen, or
    – It's a school night, or
    – Yeah, thanks, mate, or
    – Nah, I'm right, mate, or
    – I have training at 5 am tomorrow, or
          or
            or . . .

Fendix waves him away,
steers me toward the far end
of the warehouse.
C'mon, I'll show you around.

There are two large trestle tables,
covered with years of paint dribbles,
droplets from spray cans.
A thousand stories right there.

Along one side
are stacks of panels and canvases,
leaning against each other,
a clash of colour and shape.

The floor, a dark concrete,
is covered with paint of every imaginable colour,
so you'd need a cyanometer
for every shade
to match them all.

The other walls, dirty-white brick, compete
for attention with
paste-ups, stencils, paint
sprayed directly onto the surfaces.

There are small cubicles blocked with half-partitions —
studios for different artists
working with stencils, oils, cans, photography,
even embroidery.

I've only been in the place for five minutes
but I want to stay forever.

I run my hands over a stack of panels,
thickly smeared with paint.
How long have you all been here?

Well, it's Bindy's place, Fendix says,
with a nod at Bindy.
His uncle lets him use it.
It was supposed to be demolished last year
but it's still here.
And so are we.
We started painting here two years ago,
needed a place to keep everything together,
work on any commissions.

Issa comes over.
Your commissions, cuz, she corrects.
The rest of us,
we just do your fill work.

Fendix waves her compliment away.

How'd you, I ask, *how'd you start*
getting commissions?
You got to start in a group
like this, Fendix tells me.

Put your work up everywhere,
especially Hosier Lane.
And don't get caught.

Show off your stuff on socials.
Establish yourself.
Do a group exhibition.

Take your canvases around to cafes,
ask if you can hang them on walls.
Hope someone likes them, buys them.

But Melbourne –
good place to be for a street artist.
I bloody love Melbourne.

Nah, says Mack, strolling over,
just go out, spray anywhere,
forget the rules.
And go overseas, forget Melbs.
They don't appreciate us,
too much going on right now
with some of the councils documenting graffiti.

What?
Councils document graffiti? I ask.

Yeah, says Issa. *They go around the city,*
snapping pics of tags, throw-ups, pieces
on really big public property,
put them in a database.
If they catch you spraying,
and match your work up to the database,
they'll have you fined for vandalism.

Issa! Stop scaring him! says Fendix.
It's to stop repeat offenders.

You'll be alright, kid,
you're under eighteen, right?
Mack asks.

I nod.

Nothing to worry about.
They'll let you off easy if you're caught.
Hey, I'll show you how to do eyes now.

—

I know I have to go,
got to get back
before Dad and Mum are home
from their evening shifts.

I put back the cans,
thank Mack for the lesson,
snap a photo of my art
sprayed in a narrow spot
on a wall between two paste-ups.

Mack walks out with me
through that laneway of

colour, dialogue, paste-ups,

emotions, tags, relationships,

self-expression, POLITICS,

stickers, TEXTURE, pieces,

STENCILS, ARGUMENTS, art

Gotta leave anyway,
starting a shift soon, he says.

Oh yeah?
Where d'you work? I ask him.

Supermarket.
Do about twenty hours in the deli.
No school, no uni,
just work.

I stack shelves, too,
I offer. *Two shifts a week.*

He pats me on the shoulder,
clicks his keys at his car,
green P-plate clear through the back window.
Keep it up.
Boring as anything
but you'll need the money for paint.
See ya round.

I ride home,
imagining the freedom
of painting and working,
with no school.

Grace

After orchestra rehearsal in the performance centre,
Ms Liu stops me
as I'm loosening the strings on my bow,
ready to put it in my case.

Grace, do you know about the school musical,
'Fiddler on the Roof'?

I nod my head.
Yeah. I guess the orchestra
will play? So, we'll have rehearsals
as well as the shows?

She smiles at me. *Exactly.*
But instead of playing in the orchestra,
I think you should try out for the fiddler.
It's a non-speaking part, all violin.
You'd be great.

I'm stunned.
But I don't know how to act!

Ms Liu looks at me,
amused eyes.
You don't have to act, just
play your violin.

She hands me a booklet.
Here, the score. Have a go.

⎯

The score
is almost entirely
traditional Jewish folk dances,
lots of exaggeration,
an eastern European sensitivity.

It makes me want to move –
not just my feet

but my whole body,
to walk around while I play.

I play all the pieces —
the solos, the tutti sections.

Then I watch the movie.
The fiddler is this mysterious character
who comes in and out
of the lives of a small Jewish community.

There's one family
with five daughters;
the focus is on the older three.

The eldest one wants to marry
a young, poor tailor instead of an old, rich butcher.
Bad.
Her parents aren't sure
but they give in.

     The second daughter wants to marry
     an outsider, a rebel who wants change.
     Worse.
     Her parents aren't sure
     but they give in.

          The third daughter wants to marry
          a non-Jew.
          The worst.
          Her parents are absolutely sure this
          isn't right
              and
                  cut
                      her
                          off.

I think about the three Dalfinch daughters,
    expected to fall into line
        like the three Jewish daughters.

What's the equivalent
of marrying a non-Jewish man
for the Dalfinches?

A music career,
instead of an academic one.

———

Ettie had a phenomenal music career –
lighting up the way for me
with her passion, her talent, her joy.
Before her first stroke,
Ettie played her violin
as if she were
the whole Melbourne Symphony Orchestra
herself, full of string –
full of passion.

After her first stroke
at sixty-three,
she still played as if she were the first violinist
for the Melbourne Symphony Orchestra –
so much talent.

Since her second stroke
at eighty-one,
she listens to me play,
nods her head encouragingly
when I pull off a passage of complex sautillé,
slows down my tempo
with a gesture from her good hand,

blows a kiss of appreciation
when I finish –
heart full of joy.

She can't clap her hands together
anymore.

But she has more music in her little finger
poised above the purest A string
than any famous violinist.

I want to follow in her footsteps,
                    in her fingertips.

CRUX

It's 5.30 am,
I'm not properly awake,
even though I'm cycling
side by side with Dad
on our bikes.

Last night it seemed like a good idea
to ride with Dad.

But maybe the guilt I felt
about hanging with street artists
– when I agreed to this insane hour –
is not so heavy right now.

We ride through sleeping Richmond,
following the curves of the Yarra River
until we end up at Kew Boulevard,
and cycle with the other riders in lycra

up and down the hills,
around the bends.

This'll wake you up, mate! calls Dad,
as he overtakes me up a steep incline.

Dad is a wind breather.
Mum is an earth grounder.
Molly is a fire maker.
I am a cloud gazer.
    So Mum describes us.

I paint a family portrait in my head –
the four of us,
the four elements
coming out of our skin.

Dad runs two kilometres
or cycles his bike along the river
for an hour every morning.
On holidays,
the first thing he does is take his board
to the beach for a surf.
Dad feels more alive, he says,
with the wind in his face.

Mum caresses crystals –
smooth rose quartz,
jagged orange-white citrine
and spiky purple amethysts.

She talks to trees, asks them
deep and emotional questions.
The elderly white birch with scars
of experience marked on its trunk
waves its leafy arms

and gives Mum answers
about what to cook for dinner,
whether she should leave her nursing job
and study her passion, naturopathy.

Molly lights candles so frequently
she could make it a career.
Decorator with fairy lights (not only at Christmas),
lighter of candles:
tea lights along the hall table,
thick pillars at dinner,
scented ones that smell of girl,
and outdoor ones to keep away the mozzies.

She's the one who fires up the barbecue
and ignites the wood
in the steel gallon drum
when we have winter parties.

I don't talk to trees – ever.
I ride behind Dad in his slipstream sometimes.
And often,
I blow out Molly's candles
just to annoy her.

But Mum's right –
I do gaze at the sky.

You okay?
calls Dad, twisting his head
to check on me.

I give him the thumbs-up,
and he grins.

I follow his fluorescent yellow lycra
up and down the Boulevard,
back home through the streets of Richmond.

We pass one of Bindy's frightened kangaroos leaping
away from a bushfire
on the side of an organics shop.
I feel a similar panic
at the idea that Dad will discover
how I didn't
follow our agreement.
Ride a little harder,
welcome the burn in my legs.
Better than the burning thoughts in my head.

Grace

After school,
Abby and I walk through the science labs,
around the library,
to orchestra in the performance centre.
Our decade-long friendship
could be measured
        in the beat of our feet,
                the beat of our music.

Heard from your mum?
Have you asked her about playing in the bar?
Abby wheels her cello behind her
like an obedient puppy.
She always has either her cello
or video camera with her.

Nope.

Gracie,
her voice holds echoes of her little-girl self,
the one I used to swing with in Prep.

Seriously?
You're doing that voice on me now?

Abby starts to say something to me
but hesitates when she sees my face.

This is what I want more than anything.
But Mum —
of course, she'll say no.
She'll say
that she should never have let me
take my violin   *this far.*
Lessons, exams, orchestra —
distracting me from my study.

But this is what you want to do,
Abby reminds me.

I shrug. *Like that matters to her.*

Ask your dad? Abby suggests.

Well,
he'll say yes, then
he'll tell her, then
she'll say no.
And I won't get to play.
You know how democracy works
in our family — it doesn't.

Ready, girls?
Ms Liu, elegant as always in her clichéd musician black,
waves us in.

Our orchestra is a mass of checked dresses,
navy-blue sports uniforms, ponytails,
with gleams of brass and wood
between the black music stands.

I love this part of orchestra
where everyone is talking and laughing,
and the strings tune up
with sounds that should have a halo around them,
the winds blow gently through their mouthpieces
like they carry the very breath of the gods.

Abby and I slide into our spots,
me with the other first violinists.
I'm principal chair.
Abby goes to the back of the room to set up
her cello.

So grateful,
    so, so, so
        grateful
               I have an instrument I can carry, not drag.

I'm mechanical today
but no-one notices because
they're distracted, too.

Rona rumours.
More cases in Australia.

I did a quick check of the coronavirus cases
in Italy this morning.

Can't believe Mum planned her trip months ago,
allowed for every possibility,
and then she ended up in a country
with this awful virus, rising cases –
so alarming to see the news reports.

Can't believe I have two contradictory worries –
Mum might get Covid in Italy,
where there's no-one to look after her properly.
Or she might come home early and say no
to me playing in a bar.

Actually,
I'm more worried about the first worry.

Distracted or not, I know this piece so well
I could play it in my sleep.

That is actually the problem now.
Technically, I'm so good
I'm boring myself.

(I always keep my violin arrogance

                                 in

                                         my

                                                head.)

While the winds are practising their parts
I look around. We're a mixed bunch –
it's mainly Year 10s and 11s,
with the odd Year 12
studying VCE music.

Mum's already told me I can't study VCE music –
apparently there isn't room among
Chem, Bio, French, Specialist Maths and English.

All of a sudden,
I just can't bear it anymore
and I don't even know why.

There's got to be something more
than playing music
dead men wrote hundreds of years ago.

Mum and Dad want us to be
educated, yes. Academic,
absolutely. A little bit
sporty. A tad creative –
in the kitchen, with a paintbrush, invent a little
something or other.
Play an instrument, redecorate
our bedrooms with a new
cushion or photo gallery, speak with
polish, debate with flair, walk
with poise, discuss
Australian politics in one
breath while talking
about the environment
in another, throw in a comment about
a poverty-stricken nation
based on an award-winning documentary
released only last week.

We're raising you up,
not bringing you up, they tell us.
So many possibilities before you.

My parents have confused
the word 'possibilities' with

EXPECTATIONS.

—

> Absolutely not.

Mum's text is unambiguous.

> You can't go into a bar at night
> at fifteen years old
> and play music.

> It's early evening.

I plead,
from Melbourne to Milan.

> It's only for six weeks.
> Rani will be there,
> she'll look after me.

> No.
> No bar.
> You need to focus on school.
> Violin isn't a career.

> But look at Ettie!

> She was the exception.
> Look at Dad –
> he stopped playing,
> got a proper job.

> But music is a proper job.

> Not a well-paid one.

I don't bother to respond,
put my phone away.

Dalfinch daughters are always obedient.

CRUX

After school,
the Mellors' garage is full of the usuals –
the four Mellor brothers and
half a dozen of their mates.
There's a ping-pong table down one end of the garage,
an Xbox and beanbags down the other.

Finn's parents used to park their cars in here
but then they figured it was better
to park their boys instead.
Even though their house is right at the end of a court,
and they can never find
a parking spot in its curve.

I've been friends
with Finn Mellor and Sam Welton
since grade five,
when we worked out
we had the same level of footy ability,
we lived three streets away from each other,
and we all skateboarded.
Still do.

Welty likes hanging out at the Mellors'
even more than me.
There's not a crystal or aromatherapy scented candle
to be found –
instead, there are skateboards, footballs,
the scent of Lynx in every corner.
But for Welty,
who lives with his mum in a tiny apartment,
there's space and noise and people.

My garage might be for Dad and me,
but the Mellors' garage is for everyone.

Finn, Welty and I settle into beanbags,
a huge plate of nachos between us.
I paint us in my head
Andy Warhol style –
bright colours, strong outlines –
but instead of his signature boxes,
I paint us on the back of three skateboards,
side by side by side.

Finn's younger brother Jake and his mates
are batting balls across the ping-pong table.

Finn's parents commissioned me
last year to paint a skateboard
as a Christmas present for Jake.
It led to a whole lot of work
cos all his friends wanted
a custom-painted board, too.
And I repaint boards for Welty and Finn,
over and over and over.

So, I met these street artists, I tell them later,
as we muck around out front on our boards.
Mack, Fendix, Bindy.

Welty raises his voice
above the sound of his skateboard
tic-tac-ing.
Better not skate on our boards anymore.
Worth a fortune,
now that Crux is painting with the professionals.

I glide past him,
try to knock him off his board
but he's a better skater than me.

A woman walks by
with a small kid on either side of her,
one of them bouncing a basketball.

Tatts? asks Finn.

This is what we do sometimes,
we categorise random people
by their imaginary tattoos.

*I reckon she'd have a daisy
on her shoulder —
she looks kind of smiley*, I say.

Classic, says Welty.
*And for the tatt on her hip,
where no-one would ever see it . . .*

*A deflated basketball, because
she didn't make it in the Victorian team,*
adds Finn.

I tic-tac my way around the curve of the court.
Still haven't figured out
my body art yet.

                                    Spray can?
                                    Family crest?
                                    Equally important.

Grace

The audition is so easy.
I turn up, play the pieces.
Get the part.
Meant to be.

Mr Kynan, the drama teacher,
tells me to practise
walking around while I play.

It feels awkward at first
– I'm so used to orchestra-stay-seated-at-all-times –
but then it's so natural
I wonder how I sat still.

Music isn't static,
musicians don't always
have to be still.

The house is strangely empty of Mum.
Her sewing machine in the study nook
has its cover on –
usually it's surrounded by fabric,
and hums constantly.
Now it looks like a closed-up shop.

Mum always has fresh flowers in the house.
Dad complains he either has the scent of flowers
or the scent of four different types of perfume
up his nose.

Now there are vases of dead flowers everywhere
and no-one has bothered to empty them.

Sometimes I can't find a clean t-shirt
or bread for toast.

But we pivot –
the government's latest word for dealing with the virus.

It's so much easier to practise my violin –
Mum always complains
she can't hear the TV over my noise.
(*Music, not noise!* I always tell her.)

But before I start practice
I check all the Covid stats
– Victoria, Australia, Italy –
(I'm becoming a data nerd).
If the stats in Italy are a little alarming,
I play something more upbeat first.
Lately, they're always alarming.

Dad and I play violin after dinner most nights –
that never happens when Mum's around.
I tease him, tell him
that all my talent came from Ettie, not him.
Not quite true –
Dad is an awesome violinist,
he just wasn't quite good enough to play orchestra
like Ettie.

In the morning,
when I hear Dad
answer his phone to Mum,
I fling my bag over my shoulder,

call out to Mum, blow Dad a kiss,
and leave for school.

Fare thee well, my daughter,
my Amazin' Grace,
Dad sends me off,
goes back to the phone to Mum.

CRUX

Ready? asks Dad,
his video camera fired up.

I check my background is ready –
cans out, two painted skateboards in view.
My latest canvas
of a realistic blue fairy-wren
is to my left against the garage wall.
There's an orange stone
with a small scrap of paper
on top of my canvas.

Mum.

She often leaves crystals for Molly and me –
in our schoolbags, our blazer pockets,
on our pillows.

Dad reads the note over my shoulder –
Carnelian for inspiration, motivation, confidence.
He smiles. *Typical Ali Crux.*

I flick it off my canvas.

Got enough confidence? Dad jokes.

I run my hands through my hair.

They're not looking at your hair!
Dad's spent enough time
waiting for news anchors and reporters
to summon make-up artists
with last minute touch-ups
to care for my hair.

Dad gives me the thumbs-up;
I speak into the camera.

> *Street art*
> *is art without a frame*
> *borderless*
> *impermanent*
> *an act of trust*
> *a message for all*
> *a creative contribution*
> *to the community.*

> *It's respectful —*
> *don't paint over what you can't paint better.*
> *It's respectful —*
> *you have every right to say whatever you want.*
> *It's respectful —*
> *some art should be free for all to enjoy.*

> *Your views,*
> *my views — disagree?*
> *Fine with me.*
> *Self-expression matters more.*

> *But don't lump me in*
> *with someone who*
> *tags the back of a tram shelter.*

Dad stops the camera,
we watch it back.

First take,
nice, Dad says.

He plugs his camera into his laptop,
downloads it for me.

My YouTube channel
has a mix of posts –
how-to videos,
spray can demos,
my latest art.

Occasionally, Dad will film me
walking along Richmond, the city,
pointing out different pieces.

It's hard to separate Dad
from my art sometimes.

Grace

I did not sleep last night.

I want to play with Rani so bad.
I want something to change because
I can't continue to
fit in the space of
Mum's vision for me.
It's too tight, as if
I were a little nesting doll
trying to grow into her next self
without enough room.

My parents said it's fine.

—

Liv's in the bathroom straightening her hair;
maybe she's seeing Biology Ben after school.

I've still got three minutes, she says,
Don't hover.

Our bathroom is only big enough for one of us
at a time,
so Mum drew up a roster
and we are ALL sticklers
for pushing a bathroom-hogging sister out.

I don't need the mirror.

Well, that's a surprise, she says.

Forget the insult, I need her.

I need a favour.

Sam hovers by the bathroom door.
I'm next, Grace, don't push in!

I don't want the bathroom!
I want you both
to do something for me.

Two SACs this week, says Liv.
I don't have time to do anything
for anyone.

Apart from your hair, snides Sam,
as Liv sections her hair,

smoothing it in one practised motion.
Her thick dark hair is the same as mine and Sam's,
but hers always looks Insta-worthy.

I tell Liv and Sam about Rani and her offer.
I need you to cover for me,
say I have an extra rehearsal.
Thursday evening,
5.30–7.00.
In case Dad asks,
in case he's home early.

                    Please.

Liv draws in her breath.
You know you'll get caught.
Mum will find out.
She always does.

She won't, she's away.
And when she's back,
I'll figure it out, I say.

What's in it for me? Sam asks.

I'll take the bins out for you.

And bring them back in,
Sam bargains. Her persuasive skills
are on a par with Mum's in court.

I turn to Liv.
And I'll do all your ironing –
all the uniforms.

Okay, she says.

It's alright, says Sam.
We've got your back, Finch princess.

Mum never let us wear
Disney princess dress-ups.
She never let us read
the pink-and-purple-coloured books
– a dozen in a series –
with stories
about princesses who waited for princes
to rescue them.

So when we played princesses,
we rescued princes but refused to marry them,
fought dragons with homemade swords
and used the bag of frozen peas from the freezer
(meant for that night's fried rice)
as an icepack.

We were the Finch princesses,
friends to the birds,
strong rulers
of independent palaces, kingdoms, realms.
The only alliances we needed
were negotiated among each other.

(There are often three sister princesses.
        The youngest is
                always,
                        always,
                                always
                                        the most beautiful
                                                most kind
                                                        most gifted –
I often reminded my older sisters.)

'Princess' was never a term of endearment in our house
when we were little.
It was a term of power
for the Dalfinch daughters three.

CRUX

I'm stacking shelves in aisle nine.
Sugar – five different types.
Flour – six varieties.
Cooking chocolate – white, milk, dark.
There's already Easter chocolate out,
even though Easter is about a month away.

Only two hours and fifteen minutes
to finish my five-hour shift.

There are worse jobs, I suppose.
I'm glad I have the money.
I'm glad I don't have to talk to many people,
other than to direct customers to various aisles.
Not as many shoppers after 7 pm.

Welty's there in aisle three.
We got our regular shifts to line up
but they never let us work
in the same aisle
or have a break at the same time.

On my break tonight,
I stand outside to clear my head,
lean against the concrete wall
with the supermarket's logo painted large on it.

It'd be an awesome wall to spray.
I imagine an oversized cockatoo,
almost pecking his beak
into customers as they wheel their trolleys
to the car park.

Even if I were eighteen,
I could hardly spray this wall.
I'd need a commission,
someone actually asking me
to paint them something.
Something they'd pay me to do.
Wonder what Fendix would do with it.

Hanging out with Fendix is pretty much
the only way I'd ever
spray a cockatoo
on a commissioned wall.

I pull out my phone.

> Hey, Fendix,
> don't mean to hassle you but
> if you ever need someone
> to do the fills,
> wash out the rollers,
> I'd do it.

I go back inside,
unload three pallets of boxes.
Don't think about
how I'd even get away
with Dad not finding out.

I became hooked on street art
five years ago.

I always drew –
fierce dragons with mighty wings and scaly skin,
superheroes with detailed costumes,
fantastical creatures that lived in the ocean.
And birds.
            I always drew birds.

One wintry cold morning
I didn't want to go to school,
there was a spelling test,
so I groaned about my stomach.
Mum and Dad knew I was faking it.

But there is gastro going around,
whispered Mum to Dad.
Always the nurse.

Mum set me up on the couch,
handmade quilt,
empty bucket, dry toast, water.
                Watch this.

The documentary on TV
was about a group of street artists
who created murals
in cities across the world
to send out the message
that the Bahá'ís
should have the same educational rights
as all other Iranian religions.

I watched that doc
– *Not a Crime* –
three times that day.

I did not throw up.
I ate dry toast.
I submitted to temperature checks
and conversations about bowel movements.

The next day I went to school –
without complaining.

I made Dad watch the documentary.
He gave me permission to take over
one of the garage walls,
bought me some cans.

I painted my own
first-attempt,
wobbly-lined,
muddied-paint
conversation about the importance
of education for all –
even if only three other people saw it.

After that,
I saw street art everywhere.
At the skate parks with Welty and Finn,
walking down Richmond's side streets,
daydreaming out of a train window,
all over the city.

At home after my shift,
chilling out on my bed,
my phone beeps.
It's Fendix.

He invites me.
Four days' time.
To paint with him, Bindy and Mack.
Hang out in Hosier Lane,
only place to paint
where you won't get busted.

I'm thinking, thinking, thinking,
when Dad sticks his head around my door.
Hey, mate, how was your shift?

Okay. Baking aisle,
all small stock, nothing too heavy.

Great.
He steps into my room gingerly,
stepping between
discarded clothes, schoolbooks, sketchbooks.
Tosses me a couple of cans.
Two different shades of blue.
My treat.

Thanks, Dad.

He disappears, shuts the door.

It would be so much easier
to break Dad's rules
if he didn't support my art.

Corona chorus

Monday, 9 March 2020
Daily Victoria Covid statistics
New cases: 3
Total cases: 15
Deaths: 0

ZitaF
Virus? What virus?

HeyItsJye
It's fearmongering,
that's all.

SanjeevP
Seriously,
we can't hug anymore?

SafetyFirst
Better to be safe than sorry —
happy to bump elbows.

HedgehogGirl
Conspiracy theory.

LaurenQ
About time
everyone learned how to wash their hands
properly.

Grace

We're equal parts
nervousness, excitement.
Abby, Meili, Skylar and me.

First rehearsal is a scary place, says Meili,
looking around the performance centre.
Us girls clustered together in front of the stage,
the boys from our brother school
marching in down the stairs

                                  toward us.

It did cross my mind
– maybe only once or twice –
that a musical is the perfect place
to meet a guy who can at least hold a note,
a guy

              who might appreciate

                            a girl
who can play both Mozart's 'Nachtmusik'
and Queen's 'Don't Stop Me Now'.

I scan the boys
– shoving each other, grinning,
running their hands through their hair,
casually keeping their hands in their pockets –
looking with hope.

Abby and Meili are looking with hope, too,
but not Skylar,
because she's already six-months-deep
with her girlfriend, Carly.

Ooh, there's Ted, I squeal,
nudging Abby,
who carefully looks away
from her crush.

Stop it, she mutters.
Don't look.

So Meili and I look at Ted,
and Meili waves.

He's looking at you,
see, he's smiling, Meili says.

We've just messaged a few times,
it doesn't mean anything.
But Abby blushes, waves back across
the large stretch of empty seats to Ted.

Song choice for right now? I ask Abby.
It's this thing we do,
find a song for every situation.

She rolls her eyes.
Not telling.

Come on!
Otherwise I'll have to give you a song.

Fine! 'Electric Love'.

Nice!

—

Mr Kynan welcomes us all,
makes us do too many
warm-up-get-to-know-you games.

Then we start the first scene
to get things rolling,
although no-one knows their lines
or where to stand,
and we're all so awkward together,
even after the warm-up games.

At least Abby
knows what she has to do.
She's the official photographer and videographer.
She's moving around,
snapping photos of us, still in our uniforms –
not at all looking
like Jewish villagers from
over a hundred years ago
who don't have a clue
about the changes that are going to hit them.

Ted is Tevye,
the Jewish father, the papa,
and already he fills up the stage,
stomping his feet,
singing about tradition.
Poor Tevye will need to adapt
– or maybe pivot –
his ideas about his way of life.
Perhaps he could do with some training
from Dad
about flexible leadership styles.

We skip a few scenes,
and the three daughters
take their place
around a pretend washing line.

Meili is the eldest daughter,
Skylar the third daughter,
and they stand in their spot,
giggling with the second daughter, Sophie.

I'm the only musician
in this rehearsal
so Mr K asks me to play a few bars,
lead the daughters into their matchmaker song.

Meili, Skylar and Sophie sing
about their hopes
for marriage with a man
who's a scholar for Papa,
rich for Mama,
and handsome for them.

They burst into laughter
and stop singing.

Seriously, says Skylar, *these girls!*
Ditch the matchmaker –
they need to find a man
– or woman –
themselves!

Mr K laughs.
Skylar, we're talking 1905 here.
Arranged marriages.
It's about the needs of the family
over the needs of the individual.

It's fine, says Meili.
Who wouldn't want

smart, rich and cute
in a partner?
I don't think anything's changed!

CRUX

Dad wings his elbow out toward me
when I come in the back door after school
to the smell of Molly's biscuits in the kitchen.
Elbow bump?
PM says we can't hug, kiss
or shake hands anymore.
And we have to wash our hands for twenty seconds.

Ridiculous, scoffs Molly,
as she washes her hands for seven seconds
at the kitchen sink.
As if the Prime Minister
can tell me how to wash my hands.

Dad steals an orange and cardamom biscuit
from the baking tray.

Hey! Molly mock-slaps his hand.
I need all of those.
Ask, next time.

Sorry, Dad grins.
Easier to ask for forgiveness
                    than seek permission.

With biscuits, he says through a mouthful of crumbs,
looking my way.
Not relationships.
Not . . .

Alright, Dad, alright,
I don't need a lecture on respectful . . . interactions, I groan.

Smooth.
Molly pats Dad on the shoulder
and hands him another biscuit.

Grace

In our lesson at her studio,
Rani puts up her hand
to stop me mid-bow
through Tchaikovsky's 'Concerto in D major'.

What is going on with you, Grace?
She raises her eyebrows in mock exasperation.

I put down my bow in real exasperation
– with myself.

> *I know,*
> > *I don't know!*
> > > *I'm all over the place!*
> > *I don't know whether*
> > > *to play this phrase*
> > *with a romantic tone*
> > > *or an intense tone.*
> *I keep changing my mind*
> > *as to how I'm feeling.*

Rani smiles
like I'm her most frustrating student
but also her favourite one.
Your emotions
are the best and the worst part
of your playing.
Same as for everyone –
our strengths are our flaws.

I spin around, shake out my arms.
But I just don't know how
I'm feeling today!

Shaking out:
    – guilt about Mum's non-permission
    – excitement about playing in a bar
    – guilt about lying to Rani about Mum's
      non-permission
    – worry about Mum being in a country with so
      many corona cases.

Is there one word for all of that?
One emotion?
One music note?

Okay, let's break it down.
Rani demonstrates on her violin.
This piece – it's a journey,
it builds up in excitement.

Start with a lightness,
descend into that intense focus,
then glide,
glissando, glissando, glissando,
into comfort and hope.

Got it. I nod.

This time when I play, I think about
the possibilities of playing in a bar,
the journey of getting there,
the comfort of always having Ettie.

Rani smiles at me in approval.
*Don't ever
lessen your emotions in your music.*

—

When I was little-little,
too little to keep up with Liv and Sam
but big enough to feel left out,
I would dissolve
into a torrent of tears.

Mum would send me to my room,
To get over your meltdown.

Dad would sweep me up,
hold me close.
*Cry it all out,
my ocean of emotion.
So many big feelings
inside my little one.*

My sobs would subside,
my snotty nose dry up,
my ocean calm down
on Dad's knee.

I'm too big to sit on Dad's knee now
        but I'm still an ocean of emotion.

69

CRUX

On the tram into the city,
I still don't know what I'm going to do.
Get off the tram to paint
or
catch the city loop back home?

I stare at a green texta scrawl
on the seat opposite me.
This tram's pretty clean –
seats don't have any stuffing spilling out,
there aren't any other tags.

Inside the tram,
there are corporate types in suits,
shoppers with bags in each hand,
students with backpacks.

I watch one man in his thirties,
navy suit, white shirt,
talk into a phone
about a big client and a contract.
Bet the tattoo on his wrist
would be that phone,
buzzy energy radiating from it.
But maybe the tatt on his hip,
hidden,
would be his favourite childhood book,
showing him the world he could inhabit,
the person he could be.

I don't ever want to have a tattoo
full of regret
– real or imaginary –
for not taking a risk with my art.

Better to ask for forgiveness
                    than seek permission.
                              With biscuits. With art.

I get off the tram at Collins Street,
walk down AC/DC Lane,
visit the Elvis Emu by John Murray.

Fendix, Bindy and Mack are already here,
looking at the art,
deciding where to paint.

Mate! smiles Fendix.
We're gonna paint here – a quick one.
See this?
He points to a throw-up
that's been put up in two minutes –
not refined at all,
the lines are shaky,
there's no thought to the colour,
the lines fade out quickly
like the artist doesn't even know
how to move his body
in rhythm with his arm.

All about respect.
Wouldn't dream of painting over this one,
he points to Kasper's swirl of pink–yellow monsters.
Or this one,
he nods at a huge blooming flower.
Absolute legend.

You can have this bit, Mack says.
It's a smallish space
below a window, chest high.

They're already shaking cans,
putting down the background,
erasing any trace of the previous artist's work.

Don't think this guy should be too cut up,
Bindy jokes.

Doing the world a favour getting rid of it,
says Mack. He looks over at me,
standing still,
     watching.

Mate, we said quick.
I've got a shift in two hours.

The decision is lodged tight in my stomach.
It's the smell of paint that undoes me.
That chemical sniff of possibilities –
can't ignore it.

I stare at the patch of bricks
below the window.
And I can see a pigeon strutting,
greenish-purplish neck bulging,
owning this spot.

                       The way I want to own it.

Can I borrow a few cans? I ask.

Following the rules, are we, mate?
Forgot the under-eighteens can't carry cans.
Mack jeers, but he gestures toward his milk crate
of colours.

I hold my pigeon in my head,
        hold my dream to be a street artist.

Then loosen my grip,
spray – a small arc of *Battleship* grey –
fill it in,
step back to check the proportion of the head,
an egg shape in *Smoulder*
for the dirty white part of the wing,
a few black streaks.

One day
I'll have a paint named after me.
They'll call it *Crux* blue.

The others are talking while they spray
but I don't even know what they're working on,
too focused on my pigeon.

I grab *Eggplant* purple and *Hunter* green,
spray them onto the pigeon's neck.
It's step back, step forward.
I stuff up the green, take it down too far,
so tidy it up with more *Smoulder*.

I change my nozzle for orange *Eureka*,
use a skinny cap,
need something thin for the pigeon's claws.

He's actually a rock dove,
but these birds
are usually known as feral pigeons,
as unwanted in Melbourne's city streets
as Melbourne's street artists.

And then I'm finished,
keep my hands off the cans
despite my itch to feel my finger on the nozzle.

Bindy stops his spraying,
looks at the pigeon.
My pigeon.

You've forgotten something.

I scan my bird,
can't see it.

Sign it, Bindy says, grinning.

I pick up a can,
about to spray my name.
        But I can't.
        Can't admit I was here,
        can't add it to my socials,
        can't let Dad see it.
I spin the green donut around the can.

Don't want anyone to find out? Mack laughs
– at me.

The heat fills my neck.

CRUX.
    X marks the spot.
        X as a mark for people long gone
            who couldn't read or write.
          X for the nameless.
             X for the name-less.
                X for those lesser than.
             Less.
                LeXX.

LeXX.
New name.
Spray it in green
with my signature curled X.
Might need a new Insta now.
Snap a photo – for LeXX.

Hey, Fendix steps up behind me.
Great bird.
Strong lines, confident curves.
And you nailed the eye.

I just nod at him,
can't appear too excited by his words.
But maybe this LeXX
is the beginning of everything.

Grace

I've taken the bins out for Sam.
I've ironed the uniforms for Liv.
Dad's still at work –
Matt Dalfinch to the rescue
with a late training session
on leadership during a health crisis.
He won't be home until nine.

It's almost too easy.

I deliberately choose non-orchestra attire
for tonight – no black and white.
Instead, a short silky skirt and purple singlet top.

Something that doesn't signal
'fifteen-year-old girl playing her first gig'.

———

Jay's bar is on a corner,
with a glass door and large windows at the entrance,
a solid brick wall
running along the side street.
The late summer afternoon light gives the bar
its own kind of glow,
but it will fade into an intimate evening and night
as the bar grows darker,
the music more soulful,
the patrons extra appreciative.

I stop on the side street,
lean against the plain brick wall for support.
Pat my violin case for luck,
then push open the door of the bar.

Rani is talking to Jay,
who's sitting behind the piano.
He has a beard and long hair,
wears a burgundy floral bomber jacket
that screams bohemian. I want it.

We're all here,
says Rani. *Jay, meet Grace.*
Sound check, then we'll talk set list.

Jay nods at me,
Always good to have a new muso around.

Ten minutes of sound check,
ten minutes of going through the list,
ten minutes of me in the toilet.

Stomach sick,
fingers fluttering –
but not in a flexible–creative–violin kind of way.

Maybe Mum was right.
Maybe I shouldn't be here.
Maybe it's too risky.
Maybe I'm not good enough.

Rani's at the door.
Grace, we're almost on!

Usually,
Rani is the one who knows exactly what to say
before I play a big performance piece
for an exam.
But tonight,
she's too focused on her own performance.
Fair enough, I guess,
but my stomach doesn't believe that.
I walk back to the small stage,
hoping I don't throw up.

—

Abby is here.
She's sitting
with her eldest brother, Hamish,
right in front of me,
video camera on her table.
Abby can put together a mini film
like no-one's business.

She grins, gives me a thumbs-up
and already I feel better.

Jay plays some meandering chords,
the kind of thing
that non-musicians think is Beethoven-worthy
but musos know is just the warm-up.

And now Rani's smiling at the audience;
there are suddenly more people
sitting at small tables,
drinking wine,
checking their phones.

It's the phone-checking
that loosens my fear.
How dare they?
I've practised and practised
and they're checking their feeds?

Rani steps up to the microphone,
introduces the first song,
Jay plays the bottom eight as an intro,
nods me in with a smile,
and I play my first notes.

My violin dances,
Rani's voice soars,
Jay's piano notes linger –
together we weave
a set of colours so beautiful
that surely every listener's heart expands.

I stand in front of my microphone,
my five-foot microphone,

and
I
own
it.

Sometimes I stand still,
and my elbow and hands and wrists move
with a grace of their own.

Sometimes I move around,
twisting my body in time to the music,
turning to smile at Jay,
keeping an eye on Rani for her cues.

Sometimes my violin is the lead instrument,
so I give a phantom flourish,
my up-beat,
to guide Jay in.

Occasionally, I notice someone in the bar,
the way their hands curl around their wine glass,
still
for the entire duration of the song.
Or how they look at Rani, transfixed,
or look at Jay, rapt.
Or how they look at me,
a girl playing her violin.

After a couple of slower songs,
Rani nods at me,
speaks into the microphone.

*I'm going to give my voice a break,
let Jay and Grace take the lead here.*

She steps off the stage,
grabs a glass of water from the bar.

Abby crouches down in front of us,
video camera on.

Jay plays me in,
then it's all me.
All me.

I'm doing my best David Garrett impression,
imitating his cover of Coldplay's 'Viva la Vida',
until I'm not trying to be David Garrett,
German violinist extraordinaire,
but me.
I'm Grace Dalfinch,
playing a modern violin solo in a bar,
adding my own colour.

—

When I walk in the door
– no Dad yet –
my phone pings.
Rani has put $100 in my bank account.

I'm a professional.

Abby sends me the clip
of my solo
and it amazes me
that I am
            that girl.

I hum Bruno Mars's song to myself,
the one Dad sometimes sings to me,

and I picture the music video
with Bruno himself
shaping the ribbon from the mix tape,
and I feel that
  amazing,
exactly as I am tonight.

Corona chorus

Friday, 13 March 2020
Daily Victoria Covid statistics
New cases: 9
Total cases: 36
Deaths: 0

Meera
Stay at home.
Flatten the curve.

MedStudent30927
Don't wait for govt
to shut us down.
Stay at home.

Dyson'sDonuts
My catering business
needs money
from the Grand Prix.
Not cancelling.

LoneWolf
Anxiety levels – high.

SalsaDancer
It doesn't look bad now
but look how Italy started.

GraemeT
As if the Aust govt
would ever close us down.

GrandmaLorna
Look across the ditch to NZ –
that's leadership for you.

YoungYogaDad
Keep the kids at school or home?

CRUX

They're working on a commission
for a cafe in Brunswick.
It's a large concrete wall
that forms one side of a courtyard
for the outdoor area.

The cafe is only serving takeaway coffee
for the rest of the week.
There are a few customers waiting for their coffee,
standing around on the footpath, watching us.

We.
    They.

I haven't picked up a can.
                    Yet.
                      Maybe.

Fendix got himself the commission,
and has three days to start and finish it.
He invited me. Wants me
to do the fills,
then paint a magpie,
after he liked my pigeon so much yesterday.

He's all business today.
He's already sprayed out the whole design
on the wall –
a bicycle race heading
around the corner.
You can still see the markings from his doodle grid.

There are drop cloths on the footpath,
spray cans, opened tins of paint,
brushes and rollers lying in trays.

Bindy has painted the road,
Mack has started with the sky.
Issa is painting the coloured helmets of the cyclists.

Fendix nods at me.
Help Mack with the sky first –
the low bits. Watch out for
any gouges, dents, grooves.
He tosses me a spray can,
full, by the weight of it.
Fill in Mack's outline, follow his directions.
I want a sky that says blue heaven perfection,
stretching on forever.

He pauses. *And Crux,*
if anyone asks,
you're eighteen.
You're painting with me
on a commission, so it's legal.
          Somewhat.
But I didn't submit any public liability documents
about you so it's illegal.
          Somewhat.

I freeze.
I know I'm not supposed to be here
cos of Dad
but somewhat illegal?

Mack grins down at me,
perched high on a ladder.

Mate, he says, *fire up!*
Make art!

The blue paint is cyanometer 18–20ish,
I'm guessing.
I'm so tempted to pull out my cyanometer
but even though
this crew might think it's cool,
I'm not sure.
Can't share it yet.

A full can.
I spray a bit on the cardboard at my feet,
got to get the pressure right.

My hand wobbles a little as I lift it up.
I've done this a hundred times on the outside
of Dad's garage.
But this time it's for real.

My whole body moves in an arc
to follow the *tshhh* of my can
as I make my mark on Fendix's sky.

—

I'm part of the conversation
with these street artists,
my hands are covered in paint,
my paint clothes
are forever splattered in streaks of banter,
splotches of creativity,
new techniques for spraying.

I am so far into my idea of happiness
I won't find my way back to normal life.

I want this to be my normal life.

Then Fendix steps back,
looks at his piece,
beckons me over.

Okay, Crux,
I want a magpie
swooping that cyclist.
This big – he indicates with his hands.
Keep the proportion
against the helmet realistic.

So much respect in his words.

Don't mess up, kid,
he'll never let you paint again,
Mack warns, a can of beer in his hand,
nodding at Fendix.

Fendix laughs.
If it's not right,
we'll paint over it,
you can do it again.
He grins at Mack.
But, yeah, don't mess up!

Last night,
I searched through my worn, page-flicked
The Field Guide to the Birds of Australia
for magpies.

Studied
> the point of the beak,
>> glassy eye,
>>> curved feet,
>>>> span of the wing,
>>>>> invisible strength of that bird.

Sketched again.   The shadows behind.
> And again.   Lines, some feathery, some firm.
>> And again.   Negative space to hold its shape.

My magpie has a renegade attitude,
owns the sky,
courageous enough to swoop a cyclist
who dares to cross its path.

My magpie has a beak so sharp
you could carve a linocut with it,
wings so strong
they could soar without a current for days.

And Fendix likes it.
I bet Dad would like it, too,
if I ever showed him –
which I won't.

Grace

Saturday morning,
no school, no alarm, no rush.
A tennis bye
and homework that can wait.

I roll over in bed,
reach for my phone.
It's lit up
like a thousand stars.

I scroll,
     scroll,
          scroll.

Abby posted the video.

—

More scrolling.
Likes, astonishment
and a few trolls.

You look gorgeous!

Didn't know violin could be sexy.

Has she heard of make-up?

Love this, babe!

Violin girl, play for me.

Screeching cat.

Beautiful. Goosebumps.

Who listens to violin music?

You're so talented!

—

I text Abby.

What the?

Morning!

WHAT THE?

I've made you famous.
Violin girl gone viral.

I didn't want to go viral.

You are never going to get
to where you want to go
if you don't promote yourself.

I know, but . . .

There's an uncomfortable
amount of space
between our usual quickfire messages.

But what?
You got noticed for your talent.
And forget the trolls,
I'm deleting them for you.
And don't worry,
I didn't use your name.

Hate ya. Love ya.

You're gonna love me, alright.

Later, I scroll through even more comments.

Even the troll ones,
    even the lukewarm ones,
        even the bitchy ones
            can't keep the rising feeling
                of satisfaction
                    that my talent
                        was seen.

Perhaps I should employ Abby
as my media manager.

CRUX

Finn glides past me on his board,
easy up the halfpipe,
slides down again.

There are not too many here today.
Sometimes you get all the little kids
on their scooters
and you have to dodge
around them and their anxious parents.

Finn and Welty are working on their nose grinds,
I'm checking out the new pieces
lining the sides of the halfpipe and ramps.

Skateboarding and street art
are entwined for me.
Solitary practice,
doing the same thing over and over,
failing and failing and failing. Publicly.
Failing an ollie, a grind.
Failing a fluid line, a decent fade.
It's trials and tribulations,
motivating yourself, staying humble,
picking yourself up on a daily basis.
Skateboarding and street art
have the same mindset –
        you have to really want to do it.

I snap some photos
of a snake curled around a ramp.
It's the scale that grabs me –
this snake with its eat-them-for-breakfast eyes
would swallow my birds in a single gulp.

I want more space,
I want oversized, large scale, huge proportions.
I want to paint so large
the sky wouldn't be big enough for my art.

Tired of living small,
following rules,
painting the same wall in our garage
over and over.

An argument breaks out near me,
two guys shoving each other,
swearing at each other.
Welty dodges them, glides up to me.
Their voices become louder,
their gestures more forceful.

Reckon they need your dad to sort them out,
Welty says.

Yep, I say, *he's saving the world,
one troubled kid at a time.*

My voice is harsher than I mean it to be.

Occasionally, we bump into one of Dad's young men
at a park or in a city street,
and after they've hugged Dad
they'll tell me
how lucky I am to have Dad,

because he's cool, chill, knows stuff,
        and he cares.
Even Welty and Finn think Dad's awesome.

But they don't know
that Dad being Dad means restrictions and rules.

Rules about painting in the streets,
and restrictions so I don't end up
like one of his troubled kids.

It's not me that's the problem,
it's the rule-breakers, the rule-makers.

Damn the rule-breakers,
who spray private property.
Damn the rule-makers
who don't understand the difference
between street art and vandalism.
And damn the rule-followers
like Dad, who enforce the rules.
I've lived with all this for years
but now,
Dad's rules are too much.

I ride up the top of the ramp,
hit the coping and fly –
the closest I can get to the sky.

Grace

Second rehearsal,
we start at the beginning.

Even though we don't know
whether rehearsals will continue.

Mr K told us we'd carry on
until we were told to stop.
Crazy, isn't it?
To think that schools might be shut?
Probably a dream come true for some of you!
he jokes,
but his laugh is a little forced.

In the classrooms, the corridors, the sports grounds,
all of the teachers look worried.
No-one knows what's going to happen.

I'm up first with Ted.
I'm supposed to be sitting high
on a set-designed rooftop,
but for now
I'm perched on top of a ladder
with my violin.

The stage feels so large,
especially when I'm the only one on it,
and the performance centre feels even larger.

The lights will be off, Grace, Mr K says,
then the curtain will go up,
the audience will see your silhouette,
hear your music.

I wriggle on top of the ladder,
trying to find a spot
with enough stability
so I can raise my elbows,
violin in my left hand, bow in my right.

Then, Ted, Mr K continues,
you'll wheel your cart of milk in from the left,
start with your monologue.
Remember that Tevye doesn't know
what's going to hit him –
he thinks that his Jewish traditions
will protect him and his family,
ensure that everything continues on.

But we know better.
Everything's going to change.
His world will never be the same again.

From my vantage point,
I can see that all the cast and crew
in the wings
have stopped talking.

                              We all know
            Mr K is talking about more than the musical.

He shakes his head, snaps out of it.
And everyone else,
in your groups –
the papas, the mamas, the children –
ready to come in.

Got it?

Ted and I look at each other,
a bit nervous.
First up, everyone watching.

Mr K grins. *Let's go!*

Everyone's off the stage,
even Ted.

I can hear them shuffling,
coughing, giggling in the wings.

My performance,
own it, I tell myself.
Mr K nods at me.
The overture is simple, melodic.
My music fills the stage,
sets the dust motes swirling
on the wooden floorboards,
quiets the shuffling behind the curtain.

Ted pretends to wheel his milk cart
onto the stage,
stops halfway,
projects his voice over my music.
A fiddler on the roof?
Sounds crazy, no?
He launches into Tevye's speech –
Without tradition,
our lives would be as shaky as a fiddler on a roof.

I keep up my fiddle-playing,
balancing on the sturdy ladder,
but want to argue with Tevye.

Surely traditions have to evolve?
Surely daughters can choose their own happiness?
Surely our world can handle this new virus?

CRUX

My new Insta account for LeXX
has taken off.
My pigeon's there, as well as my magpie.
I put up a few videos –
add photos from my sketchbook.

Posted a new video under my Crux account,
in case Dad wonders why I'm not posting there.

Text Fendix:

> Hey, got any more fills for me?

I push Dad to the back of my mind –
art is more important than following rules.

—

Mum slides into her chair at dinner,
exhausted.

She can barely talk
after an online session
learning how to care for ventilated patients –
just in case she has to become
an intensive care unit nurse
in a hurry.

Twenty-three new cases today for Victoria.
We might have to turn
emergency departments and operating theatres
into Covid wards.
The directors are looking at Italy
and the rest of the world,

trying to predict
what will happen if
Covid affects Australia in the same way.

Mum looks worried, like
she doesn't know
what's going to happen but
whatever it is,
it's going to be bad.

Dad scoops more salad on her plate.
Less talking, more eating.
Nothing can be sorted right now, Ali.

Mum and Dad exchange a look.
I paint them in my head,
comic-book style,
faces turned to each other,
nice and close,
a shared speech bubble
in a foreign language I can't understand.

Crux, potatoes, Molly says.
Stop painting in your head.
I've asked you, like three times.

I blink, pass the potatoes
but take another one for me first.

So, what are they saying from the newsroom?

I don't have any insider info, Molly.
Everything I know, I'm filming
directly from the reporter's mouth.
No-one knows what's going to happen.
We haven't been in a pandemic before.

Dad's calm, helping himself to chicken.

Wait, it's a pandemic now? I ask.

Molly shakes her head at me.
Where have you been?
WHO declared Covid-19 a pandemic
last week.

I was pretty busy sketching magpies
last week.

Let's just eat, says Mum.
No more pandemic talk.

Grace

Mr Prime Minister,
Mr Scott Morrison,
ScoMo,
tells us
– tells all of Australia –
that aged care homes and nursing homes
have restrictions put in place
to protect the residents.
And ANZAC day plans
have been cancelled.

I care about the old diggers,
marching on canes
with shiny medals.
But I care more about Ettie.

After school, I rush to see her.

How can anyone,
even the Prime Minister of Australia,
tell me I can't see my grandmother?

Leaning back in her chair in her room,
Ettie looks at me
through purple-rimmed glasses
with tiny sparkles of gems on the side.

I hug her,
and over her shoulder
I take in her whole room in one glance.
How's she going to cope
in this shoebox
without us visiting?

Play me something.

She listens in appreciation
to a Sting song, 'Fields of Gold',
but I'm imitating Eva Cassidy's version.
I'm trying to copy the inflections
of Eva's voice with my violin.
I'm playing it with Rani and Jay
tomorrow night.

Sing me the lyrics, she demands.
I sing the first verse and the chorus.
Eva,
beautiful, too-young-to-die Eva,
knows how
to eloquently describe the human condition.

100

Ettie stares at me again.
You can sing.

I roll my eyes.
I've been in choir since
I was seven. I can hold a note.
But that's all.

Ettie snorts.
You can do more than hold a note.
Try to play a few bars,
then sing a verse, then play.

Do you know how impossible that is?
It won't flow.

But to my surprise, it does.

Ettie smiles, satisfied.
Keep practising.

She also smiles
when I tell her
about playing in a bar
with Rani and Jay.

She cups my face with her good hand.
You belong there.
I'll keep your secret for you.
And this'll pass, this virus thing.
You'll be back in a couple of weeks.

CRUX

The three of us
head to Finn's place after school,
before Welty and I have a shift.

The other Mellor boys
had the same idea –
there is a footy-sized crowd of boys
in the garage.
Lucky you can still have under 100 people
in a gathering.

Finn's mum is taking sausage rolls and pies
out of the garage freezer,
exchanging elbow bumps, jokes, laughs with all of us.
She's unflappable as usual –
if we are going down in this pandemic,
I want to go down here with the Mellor family.

It should feel as if we're having this spontaneous party,
but it doesn't.
We're noisy but there's a nervous edge.

Feels like the end of the world,
like it's the final scene
in a sci-fi movie, says Welty.

Always hopeful, aren't you, mate?
says Finn's older brother.

I draw us in my head, Mack-style –
lots of black silhouettes
against a multi-coloured, diamond-shaped background
with barbed wire and watchtowers.

I can't believe they're shutting down the schools.
Last day tomorrow, Finn says.

Everything's going to change, Welty says.
No parties. No gaths. No footy.

Mate!
Stop the doom and gloom.
You reading one of your dystopian books again?
I ask.

Alright for you guys, says Welty.
You've got garages, space, family.
It'll just be me and Mum,
stuck in our apartment.

Welty's definitely the moody one,
but he's pushed it to the max now.

Welty, says Finn, *lighten up.*

I grab one of the beanbags,
open up my sketchbook,
draw us
along a long horizontal line,
a spectrum.
Finn at one end, pulling at the line
like it's holding him back;
Welty at the other end,
the rope almost strangling him;
me in the middle,
holding a frayed rope with either hand.

Grace

Jay's bar is so quiet,
it's lonely.

Rani sends out soulful vibes
through her voice,
then changes our set list around,
choosing more upbeat songs.

Jay and I keep up,
play with spirit.

But the patrons from last week
must be buying up tins of tomatoes,
packets of pasta and toilet paper.

Because there's hardly anyone
here tonight.
Not even Abby and Hamish.

There's too much space between the tables
and not enough people.

My music career is over
before it's started.

CRUX

On the tram after school,
I convince Welty and Finn to stay on,
go into the city to Hosier Lane,
check out my art.

The city is quiet, so quiet
I almost think we shouldn't have come in –
you can feel
the lack of energy, movement
as we step off the tram.

But Hosier Lane looks like it usually does –
full of colour,
    expression,
        attitude,
            talent.

        This lane is the heartbeat of Melbourne,
            there for everyone,
          no need to pay for a gallery.
            This graffiti heart
          has space for everyone's
       opinions, dreams, words, images.
      I imagine the years and years and years
          of art in this place
           sliding off the walls,
           floating into the sky,
           creating a huge mural
            sky-wide.
         Everyone's art included . . .
     the tiny heart with the initials B.C.,
   the overblown face of a woman with tears,
     the tag sprayed in fading grey,
     the indecipherable bubble letters
        over a stencilled tree. . .
       And if everyone looked up
        to that sky-wide mural,
  they'd surely see themselves reflected back.

Today there are no people.

But my pigeon's still there,
untouched.

Welty stares at it for a while.
You've actually sprayed in Hosier Lane.
And your bird is so awesome.

I use my phone
to film some pieces,
talk about what I'm noticing.

It won't be up to Dad's standard
but it'll be something fresh to post.

I shake my head –
got to stop always thinking
of Dad and street art together.

There's a guy spraying a throw-up
– one colour,
one fluid, continuous movement,
about five letters long.

Before he begins again,
I ask if I can film him –
I need something different
for my LeXX account.

Get stuffed,
he says and moves away.

Welty grins.
I guess not all street artists
want to be famous like you.

I paint in my head,
spray an imaginary roll of toilet paper,

unfurl it across the textured bricks in Hosier Lane,
writing my new name
> new identity,
> new life
> > LeXX.

Temporarily stopped by Covid-19.

Finn nudges me. *Let's go, Crux.*
It feels weird here with no-one about.

Grace

The fish and chip shop is always crowded at this time,
Friday afternoon after school.
The smell of hot oil and fried batter
makes me instantly hungry.
Hope the government defines fish and chips
as an essential business.

But even though there are kids
in five or six different uniforms as usual,
there's no crowding.
We don't have to push our way
to the counter to order minimum chips
because there's an orderly line going out the door
with a decent space
in between every person.

After we order,
I start to move toward the door
for fresh non-virus-contaminated air,

but Abby pulls me toward the drinks fridge
because Ted is leaning against it.

He notices Abby and smiles.
She smiles back
and stands next to him
(not at all social distancing)
while he talks to her
until his chips are ready.

I stand in the awkward space
between the counter and the fridge,
try to look as if I'm busy on my phone
so that Abby can have her moment.

———

We walk slowly, eating our chips.

When's your mum home?
Abby asks, passing me her chips to hold
while she adjusts the straps on her schoolbag,
shifts her camera bag to the other shoulder.
Our bags are so heavy –
the teachers told us to empty our lockers.
It seems like the last day of the school year,
except for this feeling of uncertainty.
Hey, will your mum get back?
I mean, they're saying
the coronavirus is all over Italy.

She doesn't know what she's going to do.
Dad wants her to come back now
but you know what she's like –
she doesn't like to change her plans.

Abby smiles. *Yeah, your mum is like —*
you don't have permission to take photos of my daughters,
Monday night is pasta night,
Dalfinch daughters get ninety-five per cent plus.
Amanda Tenniel won't let anything,
even coronavirus, change her plans.

I know.
But all the stuff about Italy on the news . . .
It's the first thing I check on my phone,
every day.

Abby slings her arm around me.
Hey, your mum will be back soon,
back to managing your life.
You'll have forgotten
she was away for a month.
Enjoy life without her while you can!

I sigh.
Is it possible
to love and hate
your mum
at the same time?

CRUX

Fendix messages me.

> Got a new commission.
> Urgent
> because we don't know
> if there'll be more restrictions.
> Covid theme in the city.

The council wants something up quickly
to stop any graffiti.

Bindy and Mack are in.
Issa can help for the first day.

Are you free to help with the background?

Yeah.

Grace

Because Mum isn't here,
we have a breakfast dish for dinner.
Liv sets the table,
Sam's in charge of the toast,
Dad fries bacon, tomatoes, mushrooms and spinach
in a pan,
and I'm guarding poached eggs,
checking the whites are cooked and the yolks runny.

Totally nutritious, smiles Dad,
lots of colour, protein from the eggs.
And ready in seven minutes.

He looks almost happy,
like this is just normal,
the four of us at the table.

And since we eat it with knives and forks,
It's a proper meal, says Sam.
Even . . . she doesn't finish.

Dad's phone rings
just as we've taken our first bite.
It's Mum.
Early in the morning in Italy.
Maybe she could smell the eggs and bacon.

We're having dinner, he tells her,
putting her on speaker.
We just sat down.

What's for dinner? asks Mum,
lightly, lightly,
as if she might join us.

Sam tells her.

Oh, says Mum,
and there's a silence.
Matt, there are some containers of bolognaise in the freezer,
a couple of curries, some quiches.

I push a bit of runny egg to one side of my plate,
in case it contaminates the mushrooms.

She asks us about:
      — school tests and grades
      — screen time
      — my violin practice
      — Sam's netball training
      — Liv's work schedule
      — Griffin's worming tablet.

I think you should come home, love,
Dad says. *Safer here.*

CRUX

I'm walking home
from my afternoon supermarket shift,
almost at our place,
when I see our new neighbour, Sasha,
unloading groceries from her car
in the driveway.

A carton of eggs balances precariously
at the top of a shopping bag,
then topples out.
The eggs crack,
       splinter,
            explode,
into an abstract piece of art
on the dark driveway.

Sasha stands there
– still –
clutching the bag,
flecks of yolk on the hem of her jeans.
Here, I say,
reaching forward
to take it from her.

She clutches it more tightly, frozen.
The eggs dribble down the driveway
toward the footpath.

Her kids, two boys,
maybe six or seven,
get out of the car.
One of them skids his foot in the

runny mess,
jumps on the eggshells,
smatters them with a satisfying crack,
the other stands close to Sasha.

Liam!
The jumping kid stops moving, looks at Sasha.

This moment seems bigger than cracked eggs.
I can't figure it out
but I decide I need to do something.

I spot the hose, neatly coiled by the fence.
Hey, I'll just hose down your driveway,
clean it up.

Sasha suddenly speaks, *Oh, thank you.*
I've forgotten your name,
polite voice on,
as if she's performing for me.
I know you're Nathan and Ali's son.

I'm James.
The hose forces the eggs
down the driveway
into the gutter, down the drain.
I pretend to throw up water
over the boys.
Liam giggles, his brother scowls.

Thank you, James,
I appreciate your help.

She turns to the boys.
Quick, in the car,
we need to grab some more eggs

before Dad comes home
from the hospital, from work.

Do you want to borrow some? I ask.

I'm back with the eggs
in a moment.
She smiles at me.
Tell your parents I'll buy some more tomorrow.

Grace

I'm meeting Abby for a walk, I tell Dad.
We're going to get an ice-cream.

Dad raises his head from the couch.
Be back before dark.

I feel antsy.
The bar music from the other night still in me
but mixed up with
Ettie's nursing home restrictions,
Mum in another country,
coronavirus news everywhere.

I text Abby.

> Meet me at the corner in 5.

———

The light is that perfect daylight savings,
drifting away, early autumn evening feel.
The park opposite Ettie's nursing home

has only a scattering of walkers
and there's no-one in the tram.
Her tram.

My grandfather Jimmy
worked as a tram conductor
from the age of seventeen.
He worked his way
to driver, then scheduling manager,
then regional manager, then state manager.
He was the longest serving employee,
working there until Ettie's second stroke
and her move to the nursing home.
When he retired,
Jimmy asked the council and the depot
for permission
to place an old, unrepairable tram
in the park opposite the nursing home.

Jimmy would turn over in his grave
if he could see the amount of cigarette butts
and obscene tags sprayed on the inside walls.

Abby squints with her eyes, all pro-like.
The tram is in the perfect position
for the light.

She stands me inside the tram,
framed by the open door,
right in the middle.
The sun is setting behind the trees,
behind the tram.
The moon is already out,
a slim crescent of a nursery rhyme moon.
There's barely any traffic.

I guess everyone is listening to ScoMo
and staying home.

My violin is tucked under my chin,
bow in my hand.

Wait! says Abby,
lowers her phone from her face.
Take off your hoodie.

My hoodie?

Seriously, Grace,
take off that
baggy, enormous, fugly hoodie.

I sigh, take it off,
throw it out of sight
on a tram bench.
Pull my favourite but threadbare singlet
down to my denim shorts.
Better?

Abby nods. *Play.*

—

You can play the same song
over and over
in different environments and moods
and it never sounds the same.

Someone who doesn't know a lot about music
might not notice the difference.

But music
captures the thoughts running through my head,

the feelings flowing through my heart,
the emotions pulsing through my body.

Tonight, my song collects
        my uncertainty about the future
            my longing to see Ettie,
                my yearning to play on stage

and swirls it into my fingers,
my arms,
my elbows,
my wrists,
even my voice,
as I sing the chorus a cappella,
turn it into music for Ettie,
send that hope deep into her bones.

This song has a grace note,
a tiny note that's there for embellishment
but can easily be ignored,
not played.
Tonight, I add it in –
just because.
We can all do with an extra note
of grace.

When I finish playing,
when the last note fades into the melting sun,
Abby puts her phone down.

Lucky you've got some music talent
to make up for your lack of fashion sense.
She hugs me.
You're really amazing, you know that?

I strain my eyes to see through the fence,
past the bushes, into Ettie's room,
third window from the end.
The light's on.

Send it to me now?

Five seconds later,
I send it to Ettie,
imagine her watching it
while I watch it simultaneously.

Lucky you have cinematic talent
since you have no taste in music.

Abby – with only her phone –
has created a set worthy of a movie –
pink and gold light streaming
behind the darkening tram,
my silhouette in the open doorway.

She's moved slightly,
capturing the angle of my bow,
the pose of my body,
elbows out, arms firm,
fluid movements to play
the last lingering notes.

Permission to post? she asks.

Granted.

Abby grins.

When the clip finishes,
there are three dots under Ettie's name.

118

CRUX

Sixty-seven cases in Victoria today.
Only ten people at a gathering.
Galleries, libraries, museums locked up.
Concerts cancelled.
Offices emptied.
Gyms closed,
half the hairdressers shut.

Molly can't start her environmental studies course
at Melbourne Uni.
She has fewer shifts at her cafe;
no-one is ordering in, only takeaway coffee.
Her friend's eighteenth birthday party
is postponed.

At Mum's hospital,
the directives change every day,
almost every hour.
There's only one box of proper masks
for the whole theatre.
They had to lock up
the masks, hand sanitiser and gloves
so they wouldn't get stolen.

Dad goes to and from work, grim-faced.
His whole workplace
is entirely focused on coronavirus.

The politicians in their dark suits on TV
look as if they haven't slept for a week.
Dad's filmed the premier, Dan Andrews,
a few times this week,
giving the Victorian update.

Dad also spends more time on the phone,
being a big brother.
The teenage boys he looks after are worried –
about everything.

People have stopped hugging each other.

And there's no toilet paper in the supermarkets.
Or anywhere.
I work extra shifts –
stacking shelves to replenish
just about everything.

Customers are desperate,
looking for
        tins of tomato,
                flour,
                        pasta,
                                rice,
                                        handwash.

There's an elderly couple
with a trolley that has a wonky wheel.
He has a shirt tucked into his shorts,
long socks.
She has a walking cane.
Bet they'd have matching tattoos –
two pecking lovebirds.

Toilet paper? he asks me politely.

We're waiting on more stock.
But I can check out the back,
see if it's come in.

I come back a few minutes later,
triumphant, waving a sixpack.

Thank you, young man, he says, and
they move slowly down the aisle.

Usually,
we unpack three pallets a night.

Tonight, we all work extra hours
to unpack fifteen pallets.

Grace

Mum, still in Italy,
will have to quarantine
in a hotel when she comes back.

ScoMo has said
that international travellers
are a risk.
They're also not to be trusted
to quarantine at home.

Dad's always on his phone,
frowning.
He has forgotten all his Shakespearean lines.

CRUX

We're eating outside
– barbecued sausages and lamb skewers,
broccolini and spinach salad –
when we hear noises
coming from next door.

They moved in a few months ago
but we've barely seen them,
apart from the egg art on the driveway.

Usually, we notice Alec
leaving for work at the hospital in his new car,
crisp suit, polished shoes.
Don't see much of Sasha,
other than taking the boys to school.

Another sound.
Alec – shouting
Sasha – screaming,
                    suddenly muffled.

Dad's cutlery clatters on his plate.
He looks around for inspiration,
swoops up a handful
of Mum's homegrown lemons
from the table.

Crux, he says in a low tone,
Stand at our front door.
Just listen.

Mum raises her eyebrows.

He needs to learn this, Ali, he says.

A moment later,
I hear his sharp knock on their front door.
A pause,
then the door opens.

Ah, Cruxy, isn't it?
Alec's voice sounds smooth.
Mate, I'd ask you in
but we're about to have dinner.

Another time, Dad is just as smooth.
Brought you in some lemons.
Ali's the gardener – wonderful green thumb.
Have a good night.

Dad comes back in,
shuts the front door, locks it,
puts his hand on my shoulder.

I think he is going to say
something about respect,
bring up yet another anecdote
about his big brother work,
but he shakes his head
and has no words.

Grace

When Dad and Sam have gone out for a walk,
and Liv is studying in her room,
I creep into Mum's wardrobe.

It's the most well-organised room of the house,
and that's saying a lot.
Amanda Tenniel is super neat.
All Mum's shoes are neatly aligned,
boots on the bottom shelf, heels, sandals and runners
sorted according to heel height.
Her clothes are colour-coordinated –
all her black dresses down the back,
blending into navy, blue, purple, green, cream.
Same for her shirts, jackets.

I run my hands along
her shimmery summer dresses
in bright colours,
her woollen coats,
fluttery scarves,
dark blazers with gold buttons.

They still hold her presence.

—

I look like Mum.
We all do.
Curly, shiny, dark hair.
Short in height.

Sometimes, when I look in the mirror,
I try to work out what makes me different
from my sisters.
I try to see whether there's any of Mum in me
besides my looks.

I've seen a few photos of Mum as a teenager
– acid wash jeans and Dr. Martens boots.

Note to self –
acid wash is never a good look.

I don't know what she was like.
I read a book years ago
about a teenager who went back in time
to see what her mum was like at the same age.

The daughter was so surprised
to find out her mum smoked, ate junk food,
snuck out at night.

I don't understand
how you can go from wearing
acid wash jeans and Dr. Martens
to suits.
How you can work in a law firm all day,
looking at figures for clients,
putting together briefs full of jargon.

I slip off my trackies and hoodie.
Choose a wrap dress that says
'desk to date'.

Tie it on,
find a pair of heels,
throw on a winter coat.

I look so much like Mum
it scares me.

I put her clothes back carefully,
pull out a black, thin-strapped, tight
cocktail dress.

Transformed again
into instant elegance.

It smells of her,
and I suddenly miss her so much
that I hate her all over again
for leaving us,
       yet not leaving us alone.

Corona chorus

Wednesday, 25 March 2020
Daily Victoria Covid statistics
New cases: 55
Total cases: 466
Deaths: 0

KeepPositive
We just need to be flexible,
pivot in our business.

YoungYogaDad
One thing is true –
these are unprecedented times.

Hazza
I wish I had organised
for my bike to be fixed.

PoorMe
I've waited two years
to go on my European holiday
and today I cancelled it.

CRUX

Fendix's commission is for a three-part mural
to reflect Australia's 'essential' workers
during these 'unprecedented' times
in which we have to 'pivot'.
No-one says this Covid jargon
without air quotes.

I arrive early in the city,
double-check to make sure
I'm in the right cobbled lane.
Not many people about,
even though it's school holidays.

Fendix, Issa and Bindy call out,
Hey, Crux!

They're carrying crates of paints,
spray cans, rollers, brushes –
the usual gear.
They've even hired a boom lift
to elevate them for the top sections.

We set up
in front of three arched brick frames.
I love the texture of old bricks,
the predictable lines of mortar, but the surprise
in the surface.

Bindy starts up high in the lift,
big sweeps of sunrise colours
for his background of a doctor
coming home in the early morning
after her night shift.

Fendix directs me to fill in the background
for Mack's arch,
going as high as I can reach from the ground,
while Fendix makes last-minute adjustments
to his sketches on his iPad.
Issa starts spraying the background for Fendix.

My hands are in my pockets,
I'm trying to look
as if I'm just surveying the blank space,
but I'm stalling.

Mum and Dad were already at work
by the time I got up –
Mum's shift started early
and Dad had a breakfast meeting to cover.
I didn't even have to lie
about what I was doing for the day.

My left hand finds a small stone
in my pocket,
wrapped in a piece of paper.
Mum.
Citrine is for manifesting, she's written.
I look at the yellow-gold stone.
Message received, Mum, I think,
I'm manifesting my dreams.

Get a move on, Crux, Bindy calls,
*we only have the lift for three days,
and Issa can only help today.*

Manifesting. I spray some paint.

—

The city is a ghost town,
half the shops are shut.
It feels like an apocalypse movie.

I'd probably still paint in an apocalypse –
the last signs of life painted
on a brick wall.
Maybe a message of hope,
message of desperation.

Fendix teaches me his doodle-grid method –
using a can to spray up random letters
all over the background,
taking a photo,
using Procreate to layer his sketch
over the photo
so that the letters become a map
to line up the outline of his sketch.

He begins spraying the outline
of his frontline worker,
a teenage kid stacking supermarket shelves
with neat rolls of toilet paper.
Could be me.

The cafe commission was great,
but this, he tells me,
gesturing to the arches,
this will be seen by more people.
I want this to have a really long run.
Especially when the city's opened again.

Mack rocks up late to the wall.
Forgot the time, he says to Fendix.

130

Three days. We need every moment.
Fendix isn't impressed.
This is such a good chance for you.
I've got enough to do here,
he indicates his own arch,
can't help you. But Crux can.

Bindy sets me up in the boom lift
so I can fill in the top half
of the background in the third arch.
Night sky.
Mack'll paint a two-headed politician,
looking one way on our health,
the other on our economy.

Bindy cranks me into position.
I'm not really that high up,
only two storeys,
but I feel sky-high.
The lift is stable enough
— it's the idea of it that makes my hands shake a little.
City commission. Fendix. Bindy. Mack. Issa. Me.

But my right hand has streaks of dark *Yankee* blue on it,
the music from Fendix's speaker
fills the empty urban space,
and when I look down the lane
I can see pigeons strutting on the rooftops,
owning the city.
I'm closer to a perfect cyanometer blue
than I've ever been before.

——

When we break for lunch,
I show Fendix my latest sketch in my black book.

Fendix looks at my sketch,
looks at me.
It's always a girl, he says.
Why this girl?

———

A few days ago,
this video went viral.
A girl, my age,
playing her violin in a bar.

Mum and Dad had seen it,
Molly's friends had posted it
about a thousand times
and I'd seen it a lot.

Then another one came up,
this time
the girl was playing in an open tram,
almost dancing with her violin,
the setting sun behind her.

There was something about the girl
that made me watch it
every time the video popped up.

She played her violin
the way I paint. With

joy

flow

IMMERSION

passion

l i f e

depth

conviction

emotion

CONFIDENCE

wholeness

creativity

I watched it over and over,
sketching her eyes, her smile,
then capturing her solemn look,
elegant pose,
furious finger movements
    and I wondered for a moment
    how it would feel to have her fingers
    dancing on my skin.

—

Keep working on it, advises Fendix.
A splat of tomato sauce from his burger
lands on his shoe.

I edge my sketchbook away.

Focus on the angle of her bow,
her elbow, the lines of her neck,
the way she holds her violin.
You need stronger lines.

Can I? he asks,
hovering his phone over my sketchbook.
I'll put it into my iPad,
play around with it,
show you what I mean.

He snaps a photo, emails it to himself.

Birds, he grins, *girls.*
Wings, hands. Feathers, hair.
Not so different, maybe –
to paint.

Grace

It's only the third day
of the extra week of the holidays
and it feels
        like everything is happening
        and nothing is happening.

Mum is still away.

Dad is still worried about Mum.
He works from home in the study,
running his training sessions online.
Even more important to be flexible at work
during a pandemic.

Liv is still obsessed
with her boyfriend, Biology Ben.

Sam, still annoyed netball is cancelled,
sprays streaks of pink in her hair.

134

I'm still playing my violin
three hours a day,
sometimes with Dad after dinner,
in between learning my irregular French verbs,
doing extra Maths homework,
checking the coronavirus stats
in Italy, Victoria and Australia.

I'm still getting lots of comments
on my two violin posts.

Abby and I still text and walk Griffin.
Abby is still really into Ted.
Meili still sends us clips
from musicals every day.
Skylar is still one happy half of a cute couple
with Carly.

I still call Ettie every day,
play for her over the phone.

She's still Ettie.

> The world has stopped still,
> yet we can feel
> our frenzied, uncertain
> energy spinning the Earth.

CRUX

Day two of painting –
Issa is home looking after her younger sister
while her parents work,
and Mack isn't here,
doesn't answer Fendix's call.

Bindy allows me to fill in
his supermarket background –
empty shelves,
a metal trolley stacked high
with cardboard boxes of toilet paper.

I work in a kind of dream,
picking up the right cans,
knowing how to direct the spray
to get the dusting effect I want.

Bindy works on the kid stacking shelves,
adds in all the shadows.

Fendix makes a call
to the boom lift company.
Too expensive to keep it
for another day.
Can you hang around until late? he asks.

Sure.

As if I have anywhere better to be.

———

We're a few hours in
when Mack shows up – drunk.

He picks up a random can,
and aims it over Fendix's doctor,
laughing.
Reckon your doc's been into the meds.
Better fix her eyes, mate!

Bindy stands next to Fendix.
Together they are a mountain of anger.

Go home, Fendix says in disgust.
You can't paint like this.
Fendix leads him toward the tram stop.

Mate, I'm okay,
lemme at my cans.

Not your wall anymore, Mack, says Fendix.
He pushes him onto the tram that pulls up,
jumps back off.

Bindy walks in circles,
swearing under his breath.

Fendix stares at the blank third arch,
covered in dark blue paint
with the grid pencilled over the top.
Walks away, talks into his phone.
Pulls out his iPad,
doodles on it with his pen.

When his phone rings,
he moves away from me.

It's yours, he says, back suddenly.
Our only option with one and a half days left.
I sent the council your design —
they like your violin girl.

I stare at him, confused.

                    Mine?

Paint your violin girl.
We need to see people who make us forget
about coronavirus
as well as the people who remind us
we're deep in it.
                    Just as essential.

I pull out a pencil from my pocket,
touch Mum's stone. Grin.
Manifesting!
I'm a commissioned artist!

So, mate,
keep filling in Bindy's supermarket shelves,
I'll do the grid for you,
then you can start the outline.

In less than an hour,
I'm staring at my own arch.

Hey, maybe change
her face a bit, calls Fendix.
It'd be the respectful thing
to try and contact her,
but there's no time.
So change her hair,
make her cheeks or lips thinner —
she can't be recognisable.
And just do what you can today
with the colours we have —
I'll bring more browns, reds
for her violin tomorrow.

I check my sketch,
start spraying her outline on the wall.
Shiny blue-black hair,
singlet and denim shorts.
I'll change her lips and cheeks.

> I   C/A/N/N/O/T   B/E/L/I/E/V/E
> I   G/E/T   T/O   D/O   T/H/I/S

The violin in her hands is harder –
I stopped doing full portraits last year
cos I couldn't get the hands right.

I look over at Fendix.
He's singing, spraying,
up high on the boom lift.

Look back at the girl's hands, twisted
in a funny way around the violin.
I'm better with wings.

Hey, Fendix, I shout.

The lift lowers him to the ground,
he takes my can,
redraws her hands,
one holding the bow,
one curled around the violin.
Go paint her now.

Grace

The beautiful intensity
of Clara Schumann's 'Three Romances'

is so full on
my skin has almost disintegrated with it.
Well, at least the skin on my fingers –
there'll be new calluses on them
after this session with Ms Schumann.
Even though Clara was more of a pianist,
boy, did she understand the violin.

I shake my hands out,
rub my shoulders,
stare out my bedroom window,
then play a little Dua Lipa 'Break My Heart'
to lift me up
after all that concentration.

There were three deaths in Victoria today
from coronavirus
and now practising
for the Australian Music Examination Board exam
seems kind of pointless.

I'm aiming to do my certificate of performance
around August.
Better to do it before VCE hits.

I've discussed my plan,
my only plan,
over and over with Ettie,
mentioned it to Mum and Dad occasionally.
(*Science, Grace, you'll have the marks to study science*
or even law –
Mum's voice is always in my head).

Pass my Associate of Music by the time
I've finished school.
Study Music Performance and Music Composition

for VCE.
Study music at the Conservatoire de Paris
as soon as I'm out of school.

> Bonjour, Paris, c'est moi!

But with everything going on,
with all the focus on the frontline workers,
on who is really essential,
it feels a little frivolous
to focus on my plan.

> I want to study music in Paris –
> but we're running out of toilet paper.
> I'm nailing Barber's 'Adagio for Strings' –
> but there are burnt-out epidemiologists advising the
> government non-stop.
> I'm disappointed our musical has been postponed –
> but there are doctors and nurses preparing for the
> worst-case scenario.

> I kind of feel a little shallow now.

> BUT

> it's the musicians, the writers, the artists
> who take everything that's going on
> and turn it into
> ART.

> Essential.

Back to the plan.
Back to Ms Schumann.
Back to my own essential self.
I have enough intensity for Ms Schumann and me.

CRUX

We finish by the end of the third day,
Fendix, Bindy and me,
alone, apart from a few people
who have come back to watch us
for a bit each day.

One of them shouts at us.
What the hell are you blokes doing painting?
Fifty-four new cases today.
Go home!

But other people stop
to look at our work in progress,
ask a few questions,
apologise for holding us up.

An older guy
with a slightly lasered-out tattoo on his forearm
stops to talk to us.
I peer closer –
he's had a heart with 'Jules forever' taken off.

Why walls? the Jules guy asks.
Why not a gallery?

Art is dialogue, Fendix tells him.
Street art's a conversation
where everyone's invited.

Oh, yeah? Is that so?
It's Mack.
He's turned up,
sober, grim-faced.
Stares at my piece.

He turns to Fendix.
You gave him my wall?

Not your wall.
You didn't show up.

The kid's been painting for five minutes! Mack says.
Couldn't even do eyes
until I showed him.

Crux, Fendix says carefully,
turned up,
showed respect,
painted a real burner.

Mack kicks over a few cans,
the metal sound reverberating
on the cobbled road.
He leaves.

My hands are almost shaking,
they've been clenched around a can
for so long.
Nothing to do with Mack.
But I grab one more, a light blue.

I've been looking at my violin girl
for so long, I can't see
how I can make her
anything other than who she is.

So I add a mask over her mouth
to cover her lips and cheeks,
make her unrecognisable.
Pandemic protection or mouth taped shut?
What is her music saying that she can't?

It's an amazing piece, Fendix says.
His approval means
E / V / E / R / Y / T / H / I / N / G

I add my name, my new name.

I stand back,
look at my violin girl.

My shoulders are aching
but my body feels lit through
by an electric current.

Fendix drives me home.
Forget about Mack.
His grudge is with me, not you.

He flicks the radio up louder.
Art is hard work,
  it's a practice.
    You gotta show up.

Noted.

Here, he opens up his wallet,
hands me a few notes.
Payday.

Grace

If I kept a diary
 and if anyone from the future ever read it
  it would be the most boring diary in the world.

There is nothing going on.

Corona chorus

Saturday, 28 March 2020
Daily Victoria Covid statistics
New cases: 111
Total cases: 685
Deaths: 0

BakersGonnaBake
Starter yeast and sourdough recipe –
same day delivery in metro Melb.

GlennSmith
Fitter and stronger in isolation –
only the cost of a coffee a day!

LoveYourLentils
Here's a quick dinner
that doesn't involve
pasta, rice or tinned tomatoes –
scroll down for the recipe.

ZenMoments
Now is the time
for the Earth to pause, to rest.
Free daily meditation.

Kidscraft
30% off kids' art and craft sets
– mandala colouring, slime balls,
macrame, woodwork, gardening.

GreenToes
Can't find the food you need
at the supermarket?
Grow your own!
10% off all herb and vegetable seedlings.

HobbieFolk
New jigsaws have arrived!
500 to 5000 pieces.
Check out our new range here.

CRUX

The newspaper is read,
abandoned, recycled.
The health minister's statement
used to start a fire.
The latest celebrity gossip
scrunched to clean the windows with vinegar.
The sports section laid down on the laundry floor
to polish shoes.

Mum and Dad share sections
over the first coffee
at the kitchen table.
Even Molly flicks through it
because she has to be seen
    to be informed
        and current
           and political
now she's a uni student.

I've cooked up a stack
of egg and bacon muffins –
I'm sampling the first
when Mum calls me over.

Street art, Crux.
About coronavirus.

The muffin becomes dry crumbs in my mouth,
a potential choking hazard.

Mum flicks the paper
to my side of the table.
Page 5.

I'm there.
My art has been photographed
by a newspaper photographer,
written about by a journalist
for a state newspaper.

My art is in the paper!
My work has been recorded!
Split second –
    almost wish I'd signed it as Crux.
Split second –
    not worth the risk.

I risk looking at Dad.
He's deep in the sports section.

I squint at violin girl
with the mask over her face.
I think I've conveyed
her elegance,
her passion,
her grace.

Molly leans over my shoulder.
Ha, the toilet paper one is good.
A large splotch of her orange juice
forms a perfect pulpy circle on the violin.

My art is yesterday's newspaper already.
The impermanence of street art.

Dad puts down the sports section,
pulls page 5 close.

I hope the orange stain
distracts him
from looking too closely.

Did you see the violin girl?
he asks me.
Looks like the artist
saw the same video we did.

He holds the paper up to his nose.
You heard of this LeXX?

Nope, I say.

Check out the paper!
The Age, p 5.

> Now?
> Second week of holidays, Abby.
> I'm watching Gilmore Girls in bed.
> Third time. Priorities.

Seriously.
Grab the paper.

> That would mean
> getting out of bed,
> going outside.

Move! Now!

...
...
...

OMG!

Even with the mask,
it's you.
So you.
How do you know
a cool street artist?

I don't.

The article mentions
the inspiration behind one of the street-art pieces –
two videos of a girl playing her violin
in a bar and stationary tram.

Abby calls me.
There are three artists –
Fendix, Bindy, LeXX.
How good are my media skills?
I didn't even try,
and now you're in the paper!

How good are your Airbnb skills?
Cos I will be moving in with you
once my parents see this.
I ask,
looking at me,
    looking at me
        looking at me
on page 5 of the paper,
spread open on the kitchen bench.

Well, your mum's still away.
Hasn't your dad already read the paper?

He's gone to get a coffee,
walk Griffin.
Then he'll sit at the table
for hours with the paper.
He'll see me.
You know what my parents are like –
Dalfinch daughters are never ever allowed
to have their photo taken
to promote the school,
appear on a sports club's website,
promote anything.
Mum says you can't be too careful
with your image.

Screwed, says Abby,
pity in her voice.

—

Fendix and Bindy have quite a few hashtags –
they're part of a street art group.
But LeXX has barely any presence at all,
like he just sprang up yesterday.

I imagine slow-walking Ettie
along the brown Yarra's curves
into the cobbled lanes of the city,
pausing her in front
        – of me.

This is me
        being myself,
                playing my violin,
                        important enough
                                to represent the essential nature
                                        of art during Covid-19.

—

Have you seen this?
Dad taps the paper,
taps his phone
with my videos filling the screen.

I nod my head.
Can't deny it's me.

Dad's eyes,
equal parts admiration and anger.

You played for Ettie?
In her tram?
You played in a bar
after Mum said no?
Pride and love,
even in the wrinkles around his eyes.
Suspicion and parental concern,
even in the wrinkles around his eyes.

Nod.

Who filmed you?
Why did you put this on social media?
Mouth turned down,
squinty eyes of disappointment.
In me.

Maybe my ocean of emotion
comes from Dad.
Definitely not Mum –
there's barely a salty tear in her.
Dad's got as many different feelings
as my blue sea.

I'm missing Ettie.
She's so alone,
and I can't visit her.

So I walked there –
with Abby.
She filmed me
so I could send it to Ettie.
And yeah, she put it on social media.
For her film elective,
I add.
That's the only reason
she put it out there.

And the bar?
Dad explodes.
Now he's a ten-foot wave
of white froth and bluish-green bile below.
Look at those comments!
Do you know these people?

No!
Well, some of them.

Dad folds up the paper,
my image on the outside,
the sharp crease along my masked face
as sharp as the crease in his brow.
Tell me, why did we call you Grace?

I restrain myself from rolling my eyes.

Mum wanted to call me Talia,
but you convinced her that Grace was a name

of elegance, charm, poise, dignity.
A musical connotation,

an annotation.

Hope Dad doesn't continue to annotate my life.

Can you see where I'm going – Grace?
Not a lot of dignity in this.
Dad rolls up the paper, raps it on the bench.
Lucky your mother
is out of the country.

But even though my mother is out of the country,
Dad is not.

You're grounded.
You cannot leave the house for three days.

What?
ScoMo said we're in stage three
from Monday.
The only thing I can do
is walk with Abby.

And now you can't, Dad says.

CRUX

My phone keeps pinging.
Fendix and Bindy are rapt.
Their names
are prominent under the photos of their art
in the paper.

Their feeds are going wild,
more people are checking them out.
And they tag me too.

As LeXX.

Grace

It's because my mother is out of the country
that I'm feeling brave.

I check Fendix's feeds,
look at his posts.
Look at Bindy, too.

LeXX has no photo,
instead, a picture of a magpie.

But he painted me like he knew me.
I have stared at my grainy black and white
newspaper picture
over and over.
Looked at the LeXX Instagram post in full colour
over and over.

He saw me.

Deep breath. I hit send.

> Hi.
> You painted me
> playing the violin.
> Do I know you?

CRUX

A girl called Grace Dalfinch
messages me.
Her profile picture tells me
who she is
before I even read her message.

> Yeah, it was me
> who painted you.
> I wanted people to see
> that even if healthcare workers are essential,
> artists are, too.

> I don't know you –
> I just saw your videos.

Flicker of a second.

> You were amazing.

Flicker of a second.

Delete.

Flicker of a second.

> You were amazing.

Flicker of a second.

Send.

Her name is Grace.

Essential?
Of course the arts are essential!

Yeah, that's what I reckon.
Do you like it?
Sorry I covered your face
with a mask.

S'ok.
And absolutely, I liked it.
I was just so surprised
to see myself in the paper.

I was surprised, too –
no idea
it'd be in the paper.

Is LeXX your real name?

Nah, I'm Crux.
Can't let my parents find out
it was me.

Ha!
My parents weren't supposed
to see my videos, either.
Where do you usually paint?

Garage at home.
And art class. Yr 11.
Painted once in Hosier Lane.

I'm doing yr 11 music
but I'm in yr 10.
What'd you paint in Hosier?

A pigeon.
I usually paint birds.
Where d'you play?
Outside restrictions, I mean.

School. Orchestra, musicals.
Just started playing in a bar,
then restrictions came in.
Covid sucks!

Sucks.
I'll come and see you
when you play next.

Ok.
Glad you painted me.
Now I can tick off a life goal
I never knew I had –
inspire a street artist!

Tick! My life goal
– as of last week –
paint a girl called Grace
playing a violin
during a pandemic.

Tick!

Grace

Lockdown is tense.

Technically,
I am allowed,
by the government,
to go outside for four reasons:
 – for work or school (but our school's online)
 – for exercise (Abby lives close by for walks)
 – to buy food or essentials (chocolate counts)
 – for medical reasons (perfectly healthy here).

But since the viral videos,
I am not allowed,
by Dad locally, Mum internationally,
 – to leave the house.

Apparently, the supermarket
would be too much of a treat.

But there is no-one to stop me from daydreaming
about a street artist called Crux.

I know I'm doing that thing, that thing
where girls fixate on a guy they know slightly
and imagine up a big lovefest.

But he painted me.

I give myself permission
to crush on Crux.
ALL. I. WANT.

CRUX

First day of stage three restrictions.

Mum's at the hospital;
Dad's filming the premier, Dan Andrews.
Molly should be at uni
but she's floating around the house like me,
kind of aimless.

I sketch a bit, more ideas about Grace.
I remember that Chagall
painted floating violinists.
I sketch Grace floating in the sky,
playing her violin,
her bow a flame of colour,
criss-crossing the strings of her violin
with more colour.

I fill five pages of my black book
with floating Grace.

It's okay that I'm obsessed –
I'm an artist. I'm allowed to be.

That's what I tell myself
when I google every single
    photo,
        post,
            image,
                message,
                    word,
I can find about Grace Dalfinch.

Grace

She's coming home.
She found a flight –
exorbitant price, she said.
She's coming home
in three days,
straight to a hotel
for two weeks of quarantine.

I don't want her to come home.

She'll take over,
micromanage my homework, practice and friends,
rummage through my desk drawers
looking for evidence of mistakes,
lapses in judgement or teenage silliness –
her words.
She'll scroll through my fake social media,
mining for inappropriate use.
(Even though I only post sunset photos on it.)
She'll eavesdrop on my conversations with Abby,
gathering up information
to sabotage me,
in full lawyer mode.

Her smile will be polished,
her clothes immaculate,
and I will be trapped here
with her
until I've finished Year 12,
constantly reminded
that I am a disappointment
by Dalfinch family expectations.

And she might have the Rona.

But I want to know she's okay.

My heart is playing an allegro
at double time.
It's beating so fast,
I don't know what it's saying.

CRUX

I send Grace a text,
a casual text,
like she's just one of the girls in my art class.
Just a girl.

> Maybe
> we could go for a walk –
> got to get in essential exercise.
> Are you close to the city?
> Want to meet in front of your painting?

There's a long wait
and I watch the bubbles
of Grace's thinking,
                reflecting,
                    deciding,
until her thought bubbles form into words
on my screen.

> Sure!

Grace

When Mum arrives in Melbourne,
she has to pass through several checks
at the airport
including a swab up her nose and down her throat.

It only takes half an hour for the result –
as an international traveller
she's a priority.

She doesn't have coronavirus.

A little sigh –

        relief mainly.

She's bused to a hotel on the outskirts of the city
for two weeks.

A little sigh –

        relief mainly.

CRUX

Should I meet her
in my paint-splattered t-shirt
with grimy nails?
Is that who she thinks I am?

I think about what the girls at school
would think.

I change my clothes,
put on my favourite hoodie and clean jeans,
scrub my hands, smear gel in my hair.

Ride my bike
            to her painting.

But I stop around the quiet city corner
because my stomach is flipping pancakes
and surely just meeting a girl
isn't that big a deal.
But Grace is more than any girl.

—

She's already there when I arrive,
looking up at her painted self.

She's tiny, her painted self
looms tall over her.

Quick stab of pride –
I sprayed this.

She turns, smiles at me
and she looks kind of nervous
and kind of excited,
her hands are moving around
as she says hello
like she's trying to capture
the music in her words.
Crux?

I nod.

She's talking fast, which is great
because I don't have to say anything
for the moment.

It's crazy, isn't it?
We wouldn't know each other,
would we?

Her hands are still moving
but her mouth is still
– my turn to talk.

Oh yeah, crazy, huh?
is the best I can do.

But then I point to her painting.
So, what do you think in real life?

She touches her painted violin,
then strikes up a laughing pose
as if she's playing her instrument,
and
I want to paint
    her in front of herself
        in front of herself
            in front of herself
                like a Droste effect
                    Droste effect
                        Droste effect.

It's amazing.
My hair, the colours in the violin –
I can't believe you created this
with spray cans.

I reach up to touch her art hair
with my hand,
as if I could feel its silkiness.

And she asks me questions
    about Fendix and Bindy

                    and school
             and being at home
           and I talk back
               and ask her questions,
     my stomach stops flipping pancakes
             and we laugh
               and our words tumble over
               each other
        and create space for answers
               and
    this is me
             having a conversation
         with a girl.
                 Violin girl. Grace.

This is a moment, she says.
We need a photo. Together.
I stand next to her,
close enough to take a selfie
but not so close that I'm touching her.

She holds out her phone,
but we're not lined up properly
to fit in the frame.

I am the worst person to take selfies,
my arms aren't long enough, she laughs.
And you're too tall!

The only way we will fit together
inside the frame of her phone camera
is if I put my arm around her.

So I do,
and my hand rests on her shoulder
and she nestles in under my arm.
I take the photo,
not quite all of art Grace will fit in
and I'm sure the pancakes in my stomach
will flip themselves out
and at any moment
someone walking by will offer Grace
maple syrup, lemon and sugar.

But she stays close,
still touching my arm, shoulder, hip
while we look at the photo.
We are framed –
artist and subject and painting
together.

Grace

If the photo Crux took of us was paper printed,
it would be worn out
from all the times I've looked at it.

I can't stop thinking about
the way he touched
my hair on the wall with tenderness.

My imaginary crush on Crux
has crescendoed into forte
now that I've met him.
I add in all these new details to my daydreams –
his height,
his arm around my shoulder,
his baritone voice with warm timbres,
his sudden grin that makes his eyes crinkle,
and how he looked a little nervous,
still holding onto his bike at first
as if he needed a crutch.

And even if I knew my parents wouldn't see it
– and they've been stalking me on socials now –
I would never post this photo.
It's just for me.

CRUX

Mum works long shifts –
everyone at the hospital is worried
because there's not enough protective gear
to protect the frontline workers.

Dad works longer hours,
covering Covid news.
He films restaurant owners
who can't afford to stay open,
musicians who cancel gigs,
lawyers who argue cases
from their kitchens,
gym owners who can't run classes,

and parents who host meetings
from their kitchen tables
with kids colouring next to them.

Molly and I cook dinner together
and we don't even argue about the dishes.

All the street artists I follow on socials
haven't posted anything.
They're not allowed
to go out to paint.
Not one of the four essential reasons
to leave home.

Grace

I walk to my painting, violin in case,
stand in front of me –
two-metre-tall Grace,
full of courage and protectiveness.

I didn't know I could stand so tall.
Perhaps this is how actors feel
when they see billboards of themselves
to advertise a new movie.

I take out my violin
and play anthem after anthem.

There are a few people who walk by,
smile, clap their hands.
But it's pretty quiet.

This is me.

THIS IS ME.

THIS is how Crux sees me.

I play another contemporary song,
this one has a grace note, too.
Up to me whether to play it or not.
Musician's choice.
If I play it,
I'm adding something non-essential to the song.
Grace notes are non-essential,
mere ornamentation.
That's why they're printed smaller on the music stave,
so you can ignore them –
your choice to improvise or not
with contemporary music.

But I always choose to play the grace note.

I finish playing,
put my violin back in its case.
I namaste my hands to two-metre tall Grace.
I honour the light in you.
I will keep playing for you,
even when Mum comes home.

Although Dad calls me Amazin',
tells me I'm a better violinist than him,
claps in appreciation when I play –
he now sighs when I bring up studying
at the Conservatoire de Paris.
Don't put all your eggs in one basket, he tells me.
Not everyone's an Ettie.

You can still play,
and study something more academic.

But I have some essence of Ettie inside me
and all my Grace-ness,
my grace notes,
always, always, always
lead me to music.
There is no other choice.

———

Every morning at 8.30 –
we're not even awake yet,
it's still the holidays –
the three of us receive a barrage of texts
from Mum.

There are general ones –
who has to do what and when –
the washing, cooking, groceries.

Then there are individual ones.

Grace, remember to spend a good hour on
your French verbs.
Especially the irregular ones.
Get ahead before the term starts.

Bonjour Maman,
comment allez-vous?
See – French is fine.
Love Grace,
the prettiest and most gifted
of your three daughters.

———

Grace, did you write your history essay?
I have time to correct it
so email it today.

Hi Mum,
hope your hotel food is delicious!
Already submitted my essay –
even in the holidays.
Love Grace,
the most favoured youngest daughter.

Grace, you're on cooking tonight.
The recipe for my Thai green curry
is in the blue cookbook
with the salad on the cover.
You can use chicken, prawns or vegetables.

Hi Mum,
Going to make a slow-cooked lamb.
Already bought the meat and veggies!
Wet day today –
doesn't matter that you can't
go outside.
Love Grace,
the daughter most likely
to marry a prince.

When I was little-little,
afternoon nap little,
Disney little,
I believed I was the third sister in the fairy tales,
the most beautiful of my parents' three daughters,
the most gifted, the most kind.

It was Liv and Sam who were the ugly step-sisters
or the greedy and mean-spirited ones.
I was the special one.
One day I would grow up
and all my dreams would come true.

I just had to
            W
                A
                    I
                        T.

Still waiting.

CRUX

Molly burns bundles of sage,
waves them in every corner of the house,
trying to detoxify
the words of politicians
and the threat of coronavirus
from our home.

I should be in a pub, she chants,
    I will be in a pub,
        I am in a pub.

———

Grace texts me.
Me. She texts
                    me.

Made any more art?

A bit hard to get out now, you know, iso. Just sketching at home. Don't think street art is one of the four reasons to leave your home.

True. But art and music are still essential.

Agree. Any more random artists painting you?

Ha! Want to go for another walk?

Grace

We're not allowed to see Ettie
and she's not into Zoom technology.
Even though she's a whizz
with her mobile phone,
FaceTime is just not enough.
Especially at Easter.
She should be sitting at the head of our table,
ready to share roast lamb and Easter eggs.

So when Dad's locked
in his study for a few hours
in a crisis meeting
my violin and I go to see her.

I slip in through the service delivery entry,
past a laundry truck picking up dirty washing.

Walk around the back through the narrow garden,
text her.

Look outside your window.

The sheer curtains slip open
and she stands there –
grey pants, green jumper,
fluffy grey hair, bright smile.
And lipstick –
she always wears lipstick.

I press my hands to her window,
she mirrors me,
a little shorter than me.
And I'm short –
I'm going to be so tiny
when I'm a shrunken old lady.

I take out my violin –
I know I'm going to be stopped
but it's worth it
to see Ettie listening to me play
'Somewhere Over the Rainbow'.

No thinking,
      only feeling,
            emotions strong,
                  yearning, yearning, yearning
                  for that rainbow land
                        of no restrictions,
                              no coronavirus.

Ettie is still, hands clasped at first.
Then she pulls out her good arm
to hold an imaginary bow,

slides it across an invisible violin
to play air violin with me.

A few other curtains open,
some of the residents peek out at me.
I smile at them, they wave at me.

I've almost finished my song
when a nurse
with multiple lanyards and keys
around her neck
asks me to go.

I knew it would happen.
At least I almost finished a song.

I blow a kiss to Ettie,
pick up my case.

I'm going, I say to the nurse.

Maybe she doesn't appreciate
music or love.
Or maybe she wants to protect her patients.

CRUX

Grace and I meet outside
a corner cafe, order takeaway.
She's wearing jeans, a black puffer jacket –
just like all the girls at school
except none of the girls at school
give me flippin' pancakes.

She has a coffee
and I order a milkshake,
which makes me feel unsophisticated.
Note to self –
learn to drink coffee.
But I did pay for both of us.

So where shall we go? she asks.

I grin. *I'm going to take you
on a personalised street-art tour
around Richmond.*

Any life-sized pics of girls playing the violin?
she asks.

Nope. They're incredibly rare.

She smiles, sips her coffee,
and I could just about paint her
doing anything –
brushing her teeth, solving a maths equation,
washing the dishes –
and the paint would explode
off the canvas.

Have your parents found out you're LeXX?

Nope, I say,
wheeling my bike between us.
Although I wonder if I should swap sides
so I could bump my hip against her
    accidentally
       on
          purpose.

My dad'd kill me.
I pause.
Well, actually, he wouldn't.
He'd just be really disappointed.

But you felt you had to paint – right?
Like,
no choice, it was calling? asks Grace,
and she holds the other side of my handlebar
to stop it wobbling.

I look at Grace, and it's like
she's a music version of me.

Portrait – another floating Grace.
This time with me up there, too,
holding her hand.

What? says Grace,
and her eyes look big with questions.

Nothing, just thinking.

About what? she teases.

Nothing. My voice is mate-sharp,
family-sharp.

Grace doesn't say anything more
but she lets go of my bike
and it wobbles between us.

The silence is awkward and long and
            I don't know what to say
      and I can't tell Grace I paint her
                        in my head because
         it's weird and

                    do I say sorry, I didn't mean
        to speak like that
                            and it wasn't you,
                now I've messed up everything
                    and I can't think of anything to
say
            at all and
                    the silence is so long
                        it could stretch past
                            the Great Wall of China and . . .

Song? Which song are you practising now?
My words come out in a rush.

I risk a glance at Grace
and her head is drooping over her coffee cup
but then she looks up.

Fiddler songs. For the musical.

*So you have to play your violin
standing on a ladder?*

Yep! she smiles.
I'll have to practise my balance.

*Maybe you could play your violin on my skateboard
while going down a half-pipe!*

And now that Great Wall of China shrinks
to a single stone in my hand
and I fling it over my shoulder.

Grace's eyes shimmer
like she has a spray-painted white cross
of light in the corner of her pupils.

And if my damn bike wasn't between us
I would have reached across
and kissed her,
pancakes be battered, flattened, squashed, whatever.

We have ended up
in front of a Makatron piece in Bridge Road
and I lean my bike against the wall
so I can point out
the techniques Makatron
used to put his rhino
– massive scale even for a rhino,
lime-green and blue swirls and squares –
on this wall.

Grace listens,
asks me questions,
and when we start walking again,
I put my bike on the other side
so that our hands
        swing lightly, lightly, lightly
into the space between us,
accidentally, purposefully
        brush lightly, lightly, lightly
against each other.

And I don't know
whether it was her or me reaching out first
but we are holding hands.

Corona chorus

Wednesday, 15 April 2020
Daily Victoria Covid statistics
New cases: 8
Total cases: 1299
Deaths: 0

EduardoG
Who are the people getting Aus Post parcels?
Who has time or money to shop?
You're either working 12-hour days or on JobSeeker.

LuisaM
If I see one more photo of homemade sourdough
I'll scream.

BarbaraC
Golf? You want your golf back?
I want my father back, alive,
not a coronavirus casualty.
I want his golf friends, work colleagues
to pay homage to him at his funeral.
Only 2 of 13 grandchildren
could attend within the allocated ten.

ViMc
I'm sincerely sorry you can't go to New York
for the third time in fifteen years.
Are you sorry
I lost my hairdressing apprenticeship?

AnneS
It's sad your sixteen-year-old son
couldn't have a birthday party with 50 mates.
It's sad my 85-year-old mother,
who lives alone,
didn't have one hug on her birthday.

Grace

Abby and I are out walking with Griffin –
it's seriously the only thing
we're allowed to do.

Can't:
> – see a movie
> – eat at a pizza place
> – hang at each other's house
> – rehearse *Fiddler*
> – shop for clothes we can't afford
> – see more than one person at a time.

So, I say, *I met him.*
My voice must throw out all my feelings
because Abby stops walking,
stares at me.

Met who? Abby asks.

*The street artist
who painted my picture!
Actually, I've met him twice.
Sounds crazy, no?*
I do my best Tevye impersonation.

Abby grabs my shoulders.
You met him? Twice?

I shrug, like it's no big deal
but I am so enjoying
being the one with capital N news.

Ah, details?
And, ah, huge apology
that you're only telling me now!

Just look at his photo!
Our photo.
I pull out my phone to show her.

Send it to me, she begs.

Not. A. Chance.
You'll post it, comment on it,
it'll go viral
and even if my parents don't see it,
my sisters will,
and my life will be screwed.

Abby pouts.
You're taking away my life's purpose.
What am I supposed to do now?
Clean my room?
Play Monopoly with my brothers?

Griffin stops to sniff a tree,
circles around and around,
following a scent.

You like him, yeah?
Like like – her voice rises soprano high.
Or like like? – she lowers her voice
into a sexy drawl.

He painted me.

Like like, she does the breathy drawl again.

Griffin moves on,
Abby links her arm with mine.
So what's your song now?

'If I Can't Have You'.

Shawn Mendes, says Abby.
Perfect!

CRUX

Someone is smashing stuff next door.
Mum jumps up from the table, nervous.

Dad motions her to sit down.
I've got this.

But Mum, Molly and me
stand at our front door, listening.
Mum has her phone out.

This time, Dad's knock
at Alec and Sasha's front door sounds
less neighbourly.

No-one answers but the noises stop.

Hello? Dad's voice is loud.

Eventually, the door opens.
Alec answers Dad.
*What can I do for you,
mate?* he asks.

Sorry to bother you,
late in the evening and all that,
Dad's voice is super polite.
Just wondering if you have
a double A battery.
TV remote's not working, damn thing.
Can't find a battery anywhere in the house.

Sure, says Alec, *I'll check.*

He comes back half a minute later.
You're in luck, he says,
hands Dad a couple of batteries,
shuts the door.

Dad comes back in,
raises his eyebrows at Mum.
They spend the rest of the night
huddled over Mum's laptop,
looking up domestic violence websites.

Grace

We knew this day was coming
but it seemed impossible.

Liv cleans the bathrooms
then goes out for a walk
with her boyfriend, Biology Ben.

Sam makes a welcome home cake
(decorated with daisies),
sprawls on the couch, texting.

Dad paces,
grocery shops,
paces,
sticks eighty-five bunches of flowers into vases,
paces,
irons his shirts,
paces.

I vacuum the whole house,
practise my fiddler songs.

Ready.
 Not ready.

She turns up in an Uber.

Dad kisses her
for five looong seconds.

Hey, keep it G-rated, complains Sam.

Mum notes
 – our hair length (and Sam's faded streaks of pink)
 – the hole in Sam's t-shirt
 – Liv's over-applied make-up
 – the callouses on my fingers.

Then it's the house.
The table set for morning tea
(with a small white vase of yellow roses)
gets a nod of approval, as does
the freshly wiped bench
(with a tall glass vase of lilies).

She's grateful
— and we sigh.

Liv puts the kettle on.
Dad pulls out a chair.
Sam cuts the cake,
I plonk Griffin on her lap.

This is all I could wish for. She smiles at us,
lets Griffin slip down to eat cake crumbs.
I'm home with my beautiful family.
And I have presents!

    She opens her suitcase,
                         and it's like Christmas
        and this is what she does
           and I don't want to be caught up in it
because I still want to hate her
                for not letting me play in Jay's bar
        (even though I did)
                and I don't want to be ungrateful
     and I can't wait to see what she's bought for us . . .

Silver anklets,
        Sam: *Bags this one!*
pastel-coloured handbags,
        Liv: *Green — I love the green one!*
halter-neck tops made of silk,
        Dad: *Good grief — they're handkerchiefs!*
tiny samples of perfume in enticing bottles,
        Liv: *It smells of romance!*
lip-gloss with fancy packaging,
        Sam: *I'm even going to keep the box!*
and three carefully wrapped glass figurines.
        Me: *Oh, Mum, a violin!*

Thanks, Mum! I say, hugging her.
There is so much,
you must have spent all your time
shopping for us.

Mum's eyes are shiny.
I just want my girls to have

         everything.

——

Mum certainly didn't have everything
when she was a teenager.

We NEVER talk about Mum's past –
I've only heard snippets from Dad.

        She had nothing,
     and now she wants to give us everything.
   But our definition of everything isn't the same.

CRUX

Sunday supermarket shift –
annoying as usual but higher rate.
Welty and I meet up at the end of our shift,
unlock our bikes from the rack,
scull our drinks.

It's cold and dark
but we've spent so much time at home
we're not ready to go back now.

School on Tuesday, I say.

How are they gonna teach us online? Welty asks.
How boring is Maths at school already?
It'll be worse online.

Still got one more day.
Meet up tomorrow to skate with Finn? I ask.

Can't. Only two people can meet up.

We ride home in Melbourne's cold
and Welty's gloom.

Grace

In Science we can't do any pracs –
not really set up for a lab at home.

Pandemic project!
says Mr Gianno, beaming.
The pandemic has highlighted
the importance of scientists
– we're not just nerds in lab coats –
we're the source of data,
we're future predictors,
we're super important now!

He sets a project
on a historical or current scientist.
The usual
childhood-education-interests-successes-failures.
Blah, blah, blah.
But the main focus is creativity.

I listen to Mr Gianno's voice
coming through my screen
into my bedroom.
Still feels weird to have teachers,
and girls in my class
who have never been to my house,
see a corner of my bedroom,
even if it's carefully curated.

Professor Graeme Clark,
the scientist who invented the cochlear ear,
worked out his theory at the beach
by idly poking a spiral shell with a blade of grass.

Archimedes discovered his principle
about buoyancy by having a bath.

Now, you might think you're already
divided into logical, rational students
or arty, creative ones.
But be open to borrowing from both disciplines.
A little cross-pollination, if you will.

From her tiny postage-stamp size
corner of my screen,
Bella Ng rolls her eyes.
I guess Mr Gianno can't look
at all our screens all the time.

You have two weeks.
Full instructions under the Year 10 Science link.
Email me questions. And Bella,
use your words, not your eyes,
to express how you feel
about my science project.

Mr G's science project is ten questions long,
five marks for each. I choose Einstein.

The first eight are easy, easy, easy.
    Google.
        Read.
            Interpret.
              Type.
                  Check.

The ninth question –
'How did your scientist use creativity
to further their understanding in their chosen field?'

Google –
Einstein + creativity.

Ms Google,
source of all knowledge,
provides me with a priceless gift
 – an image of Einstein with a violin.

Stare closer.
It looks a little battered,
well worn, well loved.

And you can tell he's not posing.
The way he holds it
– he plays.

Ms Google gives me more clues.
When Einstein got stuck in his lab,
he turned to his violin to play for a few hours

to give his mind a break.
Bach and Mozart were his favourites.

And he called all his violins –
he had about ten of them –
Lina.

Love it!

I read all the links Ms Google shares.
I wouldn't be surprised if Ms Google
was singing *Hallelujah* in time with Mr G.
Because

    I get it.
        I get it.
            I get it.

A lightbulb in my head.
Maybe not as significant to humankind
as Einstein's discoveries,
but significant to me.

And even though
my violin and Crux's street art
aren't going to save lives,
I understand why we're as essential
as the healthcare workers,
supermarket stackers,
the people in suits
trying to manage the economy.

The scientists and the artists,
    the artists and the scientists.
        Both essential.

CRUX

Our Maths teacher, Mr Hullan,
doesn't show his face in our class
but talks to us, at us,
drones on in his usual monotone
and I cannot understand algebra
and I don't want to understand it
and I can't see how it will help me
in later life at all.

Finn and I keep up a string of texts.

> Reckon Hullan's tattoo
> is a sleeping kitten
> but he thinks it's a dragon.

> Nah, it's an equation
> inside a love heart.

> Not boring enough.
> It's ZZZZZZZZZZZZ.

It's raining so hard
I wouldn't be able to see the road,
let alone skate down it.

So after school,
I lie on my bed with my laptop,
watch *Not a Crime* for the hundredth time
to remind myself
there will be a time for street art.

I watch the Bahá'í students
being taught in someone's lounge room,
their faces blurred for their own protection

because they could be imprisoned
for learning,
and I thump my fist at my laptop,
and then pull out my Maths textbook,
beg Molly for help with algebra.

Grace

It's been two weeks since she came back
and the gap of freedom has closed up.

Liv hasn't seen Ben –
no need for mid-week rendezvous
in Year 12.
Sam is made to study downstairs
so she's not tempted by Netflix.
And I've only done an hour's practising
each day, instead of my usual two.
My violin is too noisy, I've been told.

Dad says he has a lot of work on,
spends twelve hours a day
running programs
behind the closed doors of the study.

Mum sets up in the tiny home office nook
between the kitchen and lounge room.
It used to be full of papers,
school notices and recipes.

Now it's her command station
(decorated with a small vase of orchids).
While she sits there with headphones on,

going through solicitor's briefs,
she comments about:

Liv's Specialist Maths SAC result,
Sam's fitness results on her app,
my French irregular verbs –
    apparently eighty-nine per cent is not good enough.

My little glass violin sits on my desk.
I've nowhere to wear my pink halter-neck top,
but boy does it look good with my jeans
or my black tube skirt.

Mum has given me so many things,
as well as my education,
but I really just want the chance
to make music.

———

I sneak out for a walk with Crux,
complete with Ciao Bella lip-gloss
and Mia Mia perfume.
Just cos they're new
and there's no point
wearing them for a school Zoom class.

It takes me fifteen minutes
to choose which hoodie to wear.
Stop. Over. Thinking. Blue.

When I see him at the top of the stairs to the river,
I forget what I'm wearing,
forget to worry about whether he'll hold my hand,
because I reach forward to hug him
without even thinking about it.

Until he puts his arms around me
and I'm thinking, thinking, thinking
about how lovely it is
and how I don't want to move away.

He shows me some of his art on his phone –
powerful eagles,
diminutive wrens,
cocky parrots,
all painted against a blue sky.

I love your birds.
And your skies, I tell Crux,
as we walk along the river.
Holding. Hands.
They look, like really look, realistic.

I try, grins Crux.

No, seriously, how'd you do it?
Mix up a bunch of blue paint?
Add different splotches?

Crux rolls his eyes at me.
That easy, huh?
Like playing a violin
is just running your bow over the strings?

I smile. *Fair enough.*

He lets go of my hand
– what? –
pulls out something from his backpack,
a rounded wheel with a circle cut out in the middle.

See?
It's a cyanometer,

an old-fashioned instrument
that some French guy hundreds of years ago
invented as a way
to measure the blueness of the sky.
His voice is gabbling,
almost like he doesn't want to give me space
to respond.
Something about how the moisture in the air
is connected to the intensity of blue.

I take the cyanometer with violin-gentle fingers,
study the varying grades of painted blue,
palest white-blue to darkest stormy blue-black.

That's so cool.
I hold it up to the sky.
Number 14 today
but it looks like it'll move to a darker 33
by the end of the day, I say,
in my best weather-girl impersonation.

Crux laughs,
and his laugh has a tiny bit of
      thank-goodness-she-didn't-find-that-nerdy in it.

And it makes me smile inside,
a happy blue 19.

Dad used to call me an ocean of emotion,
that in one day, one hour even,
I could go from calm waters to stormy waves.
Like all the colours of your cyanometer.

Crux takes it back from me.
Well, you're a musician, aren't you?
You're supposed to be emotional.

Otherwise, how would you feel anything
when you play?

And now it's my smile that has a
      thank-goodness-he-gets-me in it.

Knew my blue hoodie was the right choice.

CRUX

My phone pings,
I check it as I wheel my bike
into the garage.
It's Fendix.

> Mate,
> we're planning an exhibition
> in mid-July.
> Zephyr Studio. Music theme.
> Paint a musician,
>   a song,
>   a lyric,
>   a band,
>   an instrument.
> Wanna paint something?
> Like a violin girl?

Sure, I'm in!

Inside the garage,
I run a victory lap
around Dad's leatherworks table,
my canvases, the lawnmower.

Grace

I am no longer doing that thing,
that thing
where girls imagine up a crush
on a guy they hardly know.

Because I know Crux now.
Even though I've only met him a couple of times,
and there's only been a few weeks of texts,
I know him.
I know he is a little like me,
a lot like me,
only full of colour instead of music.

CRUX

I just need to move, to do something
to mark one day from the next,
to make my mark somewhere
rather than stare at the four walls of my bedroom.
Cases are going up a bit,
makes me edgy.

I need to connect with my city,
                    roam my city,
                        own my city.

Just two cans.
Just a couple of words.
I'm itchy.

I put on my supermarket uniform
– just in case I get caught –
leave home on my bike,
ride through the evening shadows.

There are not as many people around the station
as there usually is,
even though it should be rush hour,
everyone exiting the city to come home from work.
Every time I see a sprayed train,
I think of graffiti roots in New York,
of the bombers who sprayed their names
all over that place.

Never been to New York
but one day I will.
I'll paint there,
put my name up there.

But the station is too well-lit, too many cameras,
so I make my way to an underpass.

There are a few tags on the underpass,
some awesome graffiti with smooth-curved lettering.
I choose a spot not too far in
as I need whatever light
the quarter moon can give me.
I pull my cans out,

keep my backpack on
in case I need to leave – FAST.

My eyes start to adjust to the darkness,
I spray the letters in red first,
get the spacing right,
then use my favourite blue
– cyanometer 23 –
to outline the shapes.
Fill them in with red.

I'm working fast and focused,
never done this before,
don't want to get caught.

Can't use my phone light
in case it attracts attention –
I'm not too far from the main road,
and the police are everywhere these days.

But the thrill,
man, I understand what Mack's about now.
Quick art,
        make your point,
            write your name.

HANG IN THERE MELBOURNE

I am back home half an hour later.
I even have a bag of chips with me,
bought from the servo.

Mum and Dad are flaked out on the couch,
they don't notice my supermarket top
under my hoodie.

Needed some salt. Needed some crunch,
I say, brandishing the chips.

There's another part of me now,
out in the city,
claiming it.

Corona chorus

Monday, 4 May 2020
Daily Victoria Covid statistics
New cases: 22
Total cases: 1406
Deaths: 0

MoiraH
I'm really, really, really glad
you've cleaned your wardrobe,
decluttered the kitchen
and sorted every single piece of damn paper.
But I'm an aged care worker
and my patients are dying.

LSmith
Thanks for sharing
five easy stay-at-home make-up looks
but my bricks and mortar business
has gone digital in three days
and I haven't slept for 72 hours.

Desperate
It's so noble of you
to only support local businesses.
But I've lost my job
and I can't even support myself.

KaylaB
Quit complaining
about being at home with your kids.
I was forced to stop IVF treatment
– elective surgery.
I'm running out of time.

ChocBabe
Really impressed by your commitment to your abs.
I'm committed to chocolate cake.

Grace

Dad pulls out his violin after dinner.
Better keep up the practice.
Play with me, Gracie.
Let us play 'the music of the spheres'.

Liv and Sam roll their eyes at each other.
Their typical response
whenever Dad quotes Shakespeare.

Got your headphones, Liv?

No study tonight, Sam.

I am smug. Can't help it
if I'm the favourite daughter.

Mum watches a movie on her bed,
headphones jammed in her ears.

Dad and I play for two hours,
everything from contemporary to classic.
We don't even discuss our next choice —
one of us plays a few bars,
the other one picks it up,
our violins weave in and out
of each other,
                    seamless, spontaneous, soulful.

Some people have great memories
of playing games with their dads when they were little
but I have constant moments
of playing violin with Dad —
so many moments they're continuous.
Dad and I are always in sync.

Then we mock-argue over who Ettie
would think the better player.

Of course, Dad's good –
he is Ettie's son.
He just chose to work in HR
instead of music.
Not gonna make that mistake.

Played it safe, he told me once.
Your mum needs security.
But I have Sundays.

Every Sunday,
Dad spends his afternoons
playing in a large cafe with his mates,
a trio of violin, cello and viola.
I think it's the best part of Dad's week.
Well, it was before the lockdown.

But I want more.
I want the whole seven days of the week
to be filled with music.
That's my kind of security.

CRUX

Mum comes home
from a twelve-hour shift.

Before she comes into the house
she takes off her work shoes,
leaves them outside,
shakes her phone

out of a snap-lock bag,
puts the bag in the bin,
she takes off her scrubs in the garage,
puts on an old dressing-gown,
walks into the house,
calls out to us but doesn't let us see her,
throws her scrubs into the washing machine,
has a shower,
puts on fresh clothes,
throws her dressing-gown into the laundry,
scrubs her hands.

I just cannot use my eyes
to console patients anymore, she says.

I reheat her dinner in the microwave,
bring it to her,
mentally give her a tatt
of a nurse holding
the whole damn world
in her palms.

I'm sorry, Mum, I say in my head,
for going out painting
when you're saving lives.

Grace

Down the hallway frames are hung –
black frames,
coloured family photos –
one for each year Mum has been a mother.

She has one taken
every year on Mother's Day.

I make an appearance in her fourth one,
a bump in her rounded stomach.
After that, there are a few years
when I'm sitting on Mum's knee,
centre stage, flanked by Liv and Sam,
smiling or squinting at Dad behind the camera.
I'm always the smallest – even now.

This year,
       we stand in front of the stairs,
       clean t-shirts and trackies,
       Griffin in Sam's arms.
       Even Mum doesn't expect
       a higher standard of dress
                    this year.

We smile, we say
– *Griff-in* –
and he wriggles
as Dad snaps us.

I can't work out whether the mothering wall,
as Dad calls it,
is a display of love or control.

CRUX

Dad comes home –
he seems in a bad mood.
He's been working all over Melbourne –

filming epidemiologists speaking
outside their homes,
childcare operators
worried about keeping their centres open,
pub owners who are losing money daily.

He goes out to the garage
to work on his leather kits,
changes his mind,
comes back into the house.

He calls us to watch the 6 pm news.

*Nathan, I know you've probably done
something wonderful
but I can't take the news tonight,*
Mum says, banging a pie into the oven.
Enough of Covid.

Dad smiles grimly.
I wouldn't ask if this wasn't important.

The four of us sit through
the Covid daily statistics,
the state news,
the Australian news,
the international news.
Dad doesn't claim his work.

So it's a good news story? Molly says.

The anchor announces the next segment –
a look at the latest street art
representing essential workers.
Dad waves his hand at the TV.
This one is mine.

I don't dare look at Dad.
My heart is pounding
as the camera
– Dad's camera –
focuses on the reporter
– warm coat, lipsticked smile –
speaking in front of a city street.

The artists were commissioned to paint
scenes showing the importance
of essential workers
during the pandemic.

The camera
– Dad's camera –
focuses
on a supermarket stacker, empty shelves behind him,
and a doctor coming home from her night shift.

And we have an unusual contender,
a girl playing her violin,
but I think we could all agree
music has been vital
for our wellbeing during lockdown.

Grace's face, her violin,
are all magnified by Dad's camera.

Fendix, Bindy and LeXX
are the artists behind
these murals, the reporter says.

The segment was probably a minute.
It was the longest sixty seconds
of my life.

Dad flicks the TV off, turns to me,
brandishes my black book, open
at my sketches of Grace.

Crux. Dad's voice is harsh.
Explain to me
why I was sent to film
a good news story
about creativity and collaboration
among talented street artists
that included my own son,
who's hiding behind
'LeXX'.

I tell the truth. I have to.
Dad's figured it out –
maybe there was something about my LeXX posts
that reminded him of me.
Or maybe those curled Xs
in my signature for LeXX
were too similar to the X in Crux.
Either way,
my black book of Grace sketches
tells the truth.

Dad and Mum listen, Molly slinks away,
while the muted sports and weather presenters
smile and gesture in silence on the TV.

And these street artists – they're so cool,
and I've learned a lot.
And I met Grace,
the girl who plays the violin.

I don't want this deal anymore, Dad.
I want to paint in the streets.

The oven timer beeps,
Dad stands up, walks into the kitchen,
pulls the meat pie out of the oven,
the juices bubbling down the sides,
the pastry golden on the top.
The smell brings the four of us to the table
for dinner
but we eat in silence.

I stay away from the garage after dinner.

Grace

I'm walking with Griffin around my block
in the middle of an art class.
I have twenty minutes
to collect a handful of fallen leaves.
Mrs Hammond, blue-rimmed glasses,
scarf lover for a Zoom call,
has forgotten we're fifteen, not five.

Be mindful, she instructs us.
Be intuitive. Let the leaves call you.

Be bored, I think,
kicking up a pile for Griffin's benefit.
He buries his nose,
sniffs mindfully, intuitively,
lets the leaves call him.

I sigh and pick up a flat, brown leaf,
a few pinkish-red ones

and a yellow starfish of a leaf
with brown speckles.

Back in Zoomland with Mrs H,
we're told to choose three leaves from our collection
and sketch them.
We are to observe a similarity
between each leaf and our life.
A life-leaf connection, she calls it.

I call it weird.

But I do wonder
how Crux would draw these leaves.

One of my leaves has a heart shape.

CRUX

I hang out with Finn after school.
Can't go to his house, can't go to mine,
so we ride our bikes to the park.

It was always cooked, Finn says.
*Too many ways for your parents
to find out.*

I can't do anything, I say.
*I can't paint,
can't see Fendix and Bindy,
can't play footy,
can't hang out in your garage.*

The only thing I can do
is stare at a screen for school
and stack shelves.

And Dad's not going to
buy me cans for a month.
I'm already running low.
And I couldn't tell him about the exhibition.
I'll wait until he's forgotten about this,
tell him then.

You still have Grace.
Finn shoves me.
When can we meet her?

Sorry, mate,
no gatherings of three.

                              Got to follow the rules.

Grace

I come downstairs
to check whether Mum's reviewed my English essay.
Her request, not mine.

Mum's sewing machine whirs in productivity
with neat piles of hemmed fabric
building up beside her.

The afternoon light glows
and makes the cheap material and elastic strips
look beautiful.

It touches Mum's dark hair, softens her face,
even though she's frowning with focus.

What are you making?

Face masks.
For the staff at Ettie's nursing home.
Some staff think masks will protect them.

And this is what she does.
Just when I can't stand her,
when she's micromanaged something in my life,
she does something nice.
Want some help?

You can pin the elastic on.
She points to the edges of the fabric.

I'm not fast enough for her
but today it doesn't seem to matter.

The constant hum of her sewing machine
was the soundtrack to my childhood.
My wardrobe was filled with clothes
she'd made for me and my sisters.

A third child always wears hand-me-downs,
but mine were made with love.

CRUX

Case numbers go down,
      restrictions ease –
          ten people outside,
               five visitors to your house.

It's a huge day –
we can finally hang out together
in this cold mid-May weather.

The messages are a constant,
consistent theme:
Footy,
oval,
after classes.

We're a motley crew –
outgrown haircuts, stubbly chins.
The mullet is back,
and we're trying to outdo each other.
Welty's is the longest.

Right now,
I don't think of anything
other than using
the strength in my legs
to kick the footy, that leather pill,
propel it into a cyanometer blue, number 32 sky.

We kick until it's dark;
they won't turn on the oval lights.
Even though there's probably twelve or thirteen of us,
and there's little social distancing
– footy is a contact sport –
there's no-one around to see.

My world is finally getting back to normal.

Corona chorus

Thursday, 14 May 2020
Daily Victoria Covid statistics
New cases: 9
Total cases: 1523
Deaths: 0

SirFred
Don't care what the government says.
I'm staying at home
until there's a vaccine.

BulldogMan
If I don't see my in-laws
for another six months
it wouldn't worry me.

LoneWolf
I'm too scared to go out.

FrustratedWife
Thank goodness the golf clubs are open –
I would have killed my husband
if he'd been stuck at home
for one more day.

TanjaR
There's going to be a second wave.
You can count on it.
Not if but when.

NotAFanDan
Why is the premier of Victoria
so far behind the other states?

YoungYogaDad
They haven't learned –
they're all going back to their old lives.

ThankGodForDan
I'd rather be under Dan Andrews' care
than any other premier's.

Grace

Ettie is allowed one visitor a day
for fifteen minutes at 4.30 pm.

Dad splits the days with Auntie Laura
so we can all see Ettie. My day is Tuesday,
and once I am
sanitised, signed-in and temperature-checked
I'm allowed in.
No hugs.

I'm not supposed to touch her

       but I do.

While I tell her about
Abby,
the viral videos,
Crux,
the musical,
she doesn't take her eyes off me.
Her eyes beam love so fierce and true
it heals sorrows.

CRUX

It's still a little uneasy in the garage
with Dad and me.
He's watching me, like he thinks
I'm gonna paint outside.

       I'm not. Yet.

He's there one or two evenings
after he's finished filming
cheese and wine experts
starting up a delivery service,
teachers trying to explain economic theories
or music notation online,
landscapers who believe
they can do social-distance gardening.

Sometimes he gets an urgent call
from one of his young men —
they don't have anyone else to talk to
or there's something important going on.

Dad's voice is always so calm,
never judgey.
Wish he could lose his judgement
about me and street art.

I don't dare touch my cans
— they're running low anyway —
I just sit there and sketch owls on my iPad,
muck around with Procreate,
and hope the 90s music
puts Dad in a good mood.

—

> Sorry, mate.
> Walked past the site this morning.
> It was only your section.

The photo Bindy sends to Fendix and me
shows my art, so fresh from my hands
I still feel a physical link.

My art is now covered
with a message sprayed in neon green
sharp lettering, shadowed in orange,
over Grace's face, her violin.

END RESTRICTIONS.

No, no, no, no respect.

Fendix replies.

> Sorry, Crux.

> But your art provoked a response.
> Someone saw it, engaged with it.
> Not respectfully, but still.

> Beauty and loss.
> Temporary art.

It's just that at the moment,
there's more loss than beauty.

Grace's face — it feels so personal.

Grace

We're back at school!
I never thought I'd be so glad to be here.

Abby, Meili, Skylar and me,
we're smiling at the other Year 10 girls,
even the ones
who usually don't acknowledge our existence.

Our homeroom teacher just lets us talk.

We're supposed to stay apart,
remember social distancing rules,
but when the teachers aren't looking
we hug each other,
link arms to walk to class,
compare hair length.
(I am getting my hair cut next week
and I cannot wait!)

I saw Ms Liu throw her arms
around Ms Papadima.
I guess teachers miss their friends, too.

And we are back at rehearsals!
Mr K told us we can only have
'gendered' rehearsals for two weeks,
then we can join with the boys again.

Think of it like this, he suggests,
pacing around on the stage,
*we have to adapt like Tevye
to this new way of life,
to living with the virus.
Otherwise, our philosophy on life
becomes as tenuous as a fiddler on a roof,
balancing while playing music
to reflect our human experience.*

Deep, Mr K, very deep, says Skylar, grinning.

Want to clean out the props cupboard, Skylar?
Mr K raises his eyebrows but he's smiling.

We run through all the songs.
I play my pieces in the background
while the others do the 'girl only' scenes.

Golde, the Jewish mama,
played by Bella Ng,
sits at the table and discusses
her daughters' matchmaking possibilities
with Yente, the village matchmaker.

The three daughters sing their matchmaker song,
and I marvel at the idea
that a parent can choose their child's partner.

Then again,
I wouldn't put it past Mum.

—

Just before Covid hit us,
Liv had to choose a partner for her Year 12 formal.

Mum wanted her to choose Jake,
the son of a family friend.

Liv argued with Mum, said it was her choice.

Mum said Liv would look back on her photos
and she'd still be in touch with Jake
ten, twenty years later
because of the whole family connection thing.

Liv asked a guy she worked with instead,
a guy Mum had never heard of, let alone met.
He was at university studying biology
like Liv wants to do.

Mum said he was too old.

He's only two years older than me, Liv argued.

Mum fumed – but in her calm, controlled way.
I will not pay for your ticket, his ticket.
Or your make-up, hair, spray tan.
And I will not sew your dress.

So, I'll work a few extra bakery shifts.
Liv shrugged in her calm, controlled way.

When Benjamin Wu
 – Biology Ben –
came to pick up Liv for the formal,
she floated down the stairs
in a silver sheath of a moonlight dress
with a split almost to her undies.

Mum's face –
divided by admiration and disapproval.

Ben was full admiration.
Wow!
Kissed her cheek, led her away from us.

When Sam had extra shifts at the supermarket,
she started hanging out with a guy called Harry
in her breaks.

She started wearing make-up to work,
red lip-gloss and black mascara
to go with that cherry-red polo top.
She bought a new pair of black work pants
that fitted her a little more tightly.

When lockdown finished
she asked Dad for a lift to Harry's house –
there were five of them from work going.

Mum stood in the kitchen,
hands resting on the benchtop.
So tell me about this Harry.
School, age, what does he want to do, where does he live?

Mum didn't blink
when Sam rolled off his vital statistics.

He wants to be a tradie?

He wants to run his own construction business.
He helps his uncle with labouring in the holidays.
He's gonna finish VET,
do a building apprenticeship, study at TAFE.

Mum made Sam
complete her English essay,
iron her uniform,
clean the bathroom
before Dad drove her to Harry's
– she was two hours late.

When Mum finds out
I've been seeing Crux,
I think she'll give me
more than a dirty bathroom.

It will be excommunication.

My position is as precarious as the fiddler's.

CRUX

Another walk with Grace,
meandering without any particular purpose.
I point out some of Issa's chalk characters,
peeping out from a drainpipe,
a cluster of weeds for their hair.

We end up walking past my street.
Wanna come in?
Head – brave;
    stomach – flippin' pancakes.

Sure! Grace says, *I want to see your garage,*
where you paint.

Quick hope to Mum's manifesting gods
that my family manifest their best selves.

We don't even walk into the house,
but head straight to the garage.
Dad's there working, he looks up,
stares at Grace for a moment,
then smiles.

You're the violin girl!
After Grace has checked out
my spray cans, practice canvases,
finished pieces, the side of the garage,
we walk inside, into the kitchen.

Quick check for normal living:
Molly's music's on, newspapers scattered,
a roast already cooking in the oven – smells good –
my art leaning against a wall – a green parrot –

candles burning,
a collection of crystals, stones and leaves in a bowl
– okay, maybe a little odd but not weird –
but Mum's sculpture of a three-headed goddess
baring EVERYTHING on the table
is definitely weird,
so I take off my hoodie and casually fling it
over the sculpture.

Haven't ever brought a girl
home before.

But Mum and Molly look up, say, *Hey,*
    Grace sits down at the kitchen bench
        like she's been here before,
            Molly slides across a hot chocolate,
            Mum chats to Grace about her violin,
               Molly toasts the marshmallows
               on the edge of the grill flame,
                  plops one in our drinks.

Normal.
It feels so normal
to have Grace Dalfinch in our kitchen.

Grace

Dad and I take Ettie out, out, out
into the June-fresh winter air,
weekend afternoon perfect.

She leans on Dad's arm,
walks around the corner from the nursing home

in slow, slow, slow steps to the cafe.

But it's so busy in there
because they can only fit
a small amount of people in
– density quota and all that –
so we order takeaway.

Then we slow, slow, slowly walk Ettie
to the park over the road
to her tram.

Dad cleans a four-seater with disinfectant wipes,
we settle Ettie in,
and I kick the cigarette butts, rubbish, empty beer cans
out of her sight,
but she sighs when she sees the tags
spray-painted over the walls.

Dad and I open up
the box of vanilla slices and chocolate eclairs,
pass Ettie her coffee.

After we finish eating,
Ettie nods at my violin case.
Open that beauty up, my darling.

Dad has brought his violin, too.

It's one of those rare Melbourne winter days
where there's no wind,
you can actually feel the sun through your clothes.

We play a medley of Ettie's favourites,
and I meander around the tram
with my violin tucked under my chin.

Dad puts down his violin for a rest.
You played the grace note –
beautiful timing.

Always. I smile.

You always ignored them, Matt,
Ettie accuses Dad, eyes laughing.

I was too lazy. Dad grins.
Besides, they're non-essential.
So small on the stave –
like . . . he nods meaningfully in my direction.

Dad!
And a grace note adds to the melody,
it is essential.

Dad looks at me. *Double concerto?*
You want to play first or second?

I sniff disdainfully. *First, of course.*

Dad grins. *I would expect nothing less.*

Ettie counts us in
to Bach's 'Concerto for Two Violins in D minor',
then sits back to listen.

Our violins converse with each other.
I'm listening, listening, listening
to Dad's voice through his violin,
knowing when to respond, when to pause,
when to lead, when to follow.
I start a theme, he takes it in a new direction,
we come together in harmony.

Exhilarating.
This afternoon is exhilarating
and I want to remember it forever.

—

After we have taken Ettie back
to the home,
Dad and I amble to the car, drive home.

Dad, I ask,
taking advantage of this mellow moment,
Why doesn't Mum want me
to make violin my career?
Why does she want me
to do so well in school
when all I really want is to play my violin,
become a musician?

Dad's hands are steady on the wheel,
and he doesn't look at me.

Your mum wants you to have security,
to earn enough money to look after yourself.
She's not so sure that playing your violin in bars
will get you very far.

I'm good enough, Dad.
He knows I'm not boasting.

I know you're good, darling,
but I want you to have a plan B.

If you have a plan B,
you're not committed enough to plan A.
Plan A is the plan, I snap back.

You know, Dad says,
Mum is exactly the same. No plan B.
She got herself an education,
then a job, then a family.
That was the plan.

Then he quotes a Shakespeare line at me –
'Thou art thy mother's glass,
And she in thee.'

I shiver.

    I

        do

            not

                want

                    to

                        be

                            like

                                Mum.

Dad notices the way I recoil.
Mum is not the enemy, he retorts.
Who took you to violin lessons in primary school?
Who turns up to every orchestra concert?
Who buys you sheet music, takes your bow to be re-strung?
Mum just wants you to have options.

Okay, you're right, I'm sorry.
But my voice doesn't exactly
share the same depth
as a note on the D string.

No exhilaration left now.

CRUX

Fendix texts me.

> Come over to the warehouse tomorrow,
> paint and pizza.

I stare at my phone.
Is this allowed?
By the state, still watching Covid stats,
creeping up high in early July?
By Dad, still watching me?

Gotta do the right thing.
There were seventy-three cases today.

I find Dad outside, weeding.

So, Fendix just invited me
to his warehouse to paint.
Okay?

Dad straightens up.
Definitely at the warehouse?
Nowhere else?

Paint and pizza at the warehouse.
Legit.

Alright, go paint.

Grace

The four of us are sitting in a booth
at Meili's local Mexican place.
Skylar shows off a new necklace from her girlfriend,
Abby films the Mexican hats hung on the wall,
Meili points to the chocolate dessert on the menu
and I smile, soak up
my friends' presence like it's sunlight.

We hold up our drinks.
To the end of Covid!
To the end of staying at home!
To the beginning of the musical again!
To the afterparty!

It doesn't seem that bad
now that we're out, Meili says.
It's like things just stopped for a bit,
and now everything is back to
normal.

CRUX

At the warehouse, Fendix lets me in.
Crux!
and the way he says my name
is an invitation to belong here.

Bindy and Issa are already there,
leaning over one of the tables,
sketching in their black books.

For the next hour,
we check out each other's books,
argue about the music,
plan out the exhibition,
and Fendix tells us about a commission
he's applied for in Brunswick.

After pizza, we swap books,
work in pencil or fine marker.

These books will be worth
a fortune in twenty years' time, jokes Bindy.

I draw an owl in Fendix's book,
a blue fairy-wren for Issa,
then start flicking through Bindy's book
for a spare page.
I'll give him an eagle.

My eagle dominates the page,
wings spread, he owns the sky.

The warehouse door opens
and thuds back against the wall.
Mack swarms in like he owns the place,
swipes a piece of pizza – on his third attempt,
opens up one of his beers – on his second attempt,
offers me one.

I shake my head.
He's turned into one of his dark figures
on the wall – enigmatic.

Got to follow the rules,
hey mate? he slurs,

falls into an empty chair next to me,
his head slumping into his chest.

So many conversations with Dad
about alcohol,
holding it well, getting messy,
knowing when to stop, looking after your mates,
happy drunks, sloppy drunks, confessional drunks,
angry drunks, spewing drunks,
and here I am,
with no idea how to answer Mack.

Get a grip, says Fendix,
pushing the half-eaten pizza away from him.
Go sleep it off.
He gestures to the couch in the back corner.

Nah, says Mack, head jerking up.
He leans over my eagle, spills his beer on it.
A brown stain fills the outline of one wing.
It almost looks like a delicate watercolour
but it's too pretty for an eagle,
too subtle for Mack.

Get it together or go home, says Bindy,
blotting up the beer-stained page with his sleeve,
my eagle still marked faintly with Mack's drink.

Gonna make me?
asks Mack, leaning back,
one leg balancing on the other knee,
the chair tipped back precariously.

Yeah, says Bindy.
My warehouse, my rules. Go.

You're just another rules person.
Covid rules, warehouse rules.
Mack is standing up now,
gripping the table knuckle-strong with one hand,
holding his beer with the other.

And you, he says,
pointing to me with his unsteady beer hand,
you should never have painted that wall.
Not good enough.
That was my wall.
He pauses, smiles. *At least it's mine now.*

I stand up, confused,
mouth goldfish-open.

I gave that wall to Crux, says Fendix,
nothing to do with him.

Wait, Issa says.
It was you who sprayed Crux's piece?

Yeah, Crux's piece on MY wall, says Mack,
beer sloshing out of his bottle.
Not his, mine.

He shoves me but I stand fixed
and he steps away.

I'm fixed –
not because I'm standing up to him
but because my feet can't move
while I take it all in.

Mack tagged my work?

Mack is staggering now.
No more lockdowns, he mutters.
No more restrictions.
Doesn't matter if there are more cases now.
Can't shut us up again.

Fendix grabs Mack around the shoulders,
steers him toward the door,
pushes him out.

I'm sorry, Crux, says Issa.

My face needs a flame-red-hot cyanometer
to record the emotions flushing through me.

Sirum black-red
     Denial – didn't happen.

Chilli
     Shock – how could this happen?

Pepper
     Doubt – there must be some mistake.

Soviet
     Reality – this really did happen.

Matador
     Slow burn anger – what sort of person does this?

Power
     Fury – how dare he?

Red, red, red.
Red is the colour of
R / A / G / E

Grace

At the nursing home,
Helena and her posse of wilted women
are waiting at the door again.

I guess they don't know it's the school holidays,
no imaginary children to wait for now.

I start to hug Helena,
but then I realise I shouldn't,
do an awkward shuffle back.

Down the lino corridor,
left past the nurse's station, another long corridor,
handrails on either side, right past the lounge room,
into Ettie's room.

Darling! she calls out
from her chair by the window.

She always looks out to the park, to her tram,
as if Jimmy is somewhere there,
perhaps standing in the doorway.

Talk with me while you tune up.
She nods at my violin.

I smile. *So hard to choose, Ettie –*
talking with you or playing for you.

We can do both. She smiles back.
But first, play me something magnificent.
And sing it.

I play 'Hallelujah' –
so many versions,

so many artists experimenting
with the mighty Leonard Cohen's words and lyrics.

The background noises of the nursing home –
trolleys squeaking on lino floors,
staff talking in loud voices,
doors opening and closing – fade away
because this song is truly majestic
and even though no-one understands all the words,
it contains enough joy and pathos
to make everyone stop for a moment
and feel

SOMETHING.

Beautiful.
Ettie smiles, touches my hand.

This is the last time
I can see you for a while, I say.
191 cases today.
Another lockdown,
but maybe not as long this time.

Suddenly, Ettie looks sad
and lonely and smaller.

Just keep playing.
Play for me. Play for you.

You know I want to play contemporary,
not classical, right? I remind her.
Not like you.

Ettie looks indignant.
I don't mind what you play, darling,

just play.
It's your gift – use it your way.

I kiss her soft cheek,
breathe in essence of Ettie.
Well, you passed the gift to me.

Ettie smiles. *Now go back out*
and conquer the world.

CRUX

Another Grace walk.
She can't come over this time,
back to lockdown restrictions.

When I heard we were going back into lockdown,
I mentally sprayed a red cross
over my latest Grace sketch.
Don't know when
I'll get to paint her for the exhibition.

I am already painting her in my head
when she arrives at the corner cafe.

So many destructive people out there, she says,
after I tell her about Mack and her mural.

Don't go and look at it.
Otherwise it will spoil
your own image of yourself.
Wish I could fix it up.
Fendix said he won't carry cans

with him at the moment – too many police.
He'd look like a tagger, not an artist.

I thought it was over, she says,
holding my hand as we walk
because this is just what we do now,
and the warmth of her skin
still sends pulses of light through me.
Covid done, back to normal.
I know everyone is missing out.
But I'm missing out
on seeing Ettie, the musical,
and my violin exam has been postponed.
And remote learning sucks.
Six weeks of this –
I don't know how I'm going to do it.

Here, I say, fishing in my pocket,
an amethyst.

Grace blinks in surprise
as I put it into her hand.

My mum is really into crystals.
She always puts them in our pockets.

I don't tell Grace
about the notes she puts in with them.

I think this one represents
calmness. Keep it.

She tucks the crystal into her hand,
and I put my hand over hers.
I curl my fingernails inward.
Sorry, my nails always have paint flakes.

She laughs, holds out her hand,
fingers into her palm.
My nails are always short and stubby
for violin.
I never get them painted. Never wear rings.
She sighs dramatically.
The things I have to give up for my art.

I laugh,
and the moment is easy,
and she reaches up,
stands on tiptoes,
stretches her arms around my neck,
tucks her head into my shoulder.

I can smell her shampoo,
feel the softness of her hair under my chin.
I wrap my arms around her
and we stand so still
as if we were stationary figures painted on a wall.

I am wondering, wondering, wondering
whether this could be the perfect moment,
the perfect moment to kiss her
but she pulls back
and her face is so sad.

Hey, it will be alright.
We got through it the last time.
And we can still see each other,
go for walks.
I really, really
wish that I could bend my head down
to hers
but there's too much space

between us now
and it doesn't seem like the right moment.

I know.
But sometimes it's hard to sneak out.
I haven't told my parents about you.
Mum'd freak out.

Huh? I raise my eyebrows.
I thought I was arty weird,
not scare-the-parents weird.

She punches me lightly on the arm.
I don't think you're weird.
But my mum,
she's sooo . . . she's sooo straight, conservative,
she's into good grades,
wants me to get a high ATAR.
She was really tough on my sisters
when they brought boyfriends home.
She doesn't want any of us to be distracted.

I can be undistracting.
And I am wondering, wondering, wondering
whether Grace has just said
– maybe not in exact words –
that I'm her boyfriend?

But Grace throws her head up and laughs,
and I bend my head down
but she looks away again.
So I can't tell her about you.
Especially not after you painted me.
My parents don't even approve
of my photo being in the school newsletter,
let alone on a city wall!

She draws breath but looks sad again.
I've just got to wait it out,
finish Year 12, move out,
study music overseas.

Thanks for the crystal,
she stretches up on her toes,
kisses me softly on the cheek,
walks away.

Maybe it was
the perfect moment
and I missed it.

Corona chorus

Wednesday, 8 July 2020
Daily Victoria Covid statistics
New cases: 134
Total cases: 2942
Deaths: 0

LoneWolf
I can't do this,
I just can't.

TiredMum
Why is it happening to Victoria?

Furious
Do not tell me
to pivot
again.

Grace

All the school meetings are online now.
Mum and Dad have three nights in a row
where they sit at the kitchen table
in front of their laptops.

Monday is all about Liv
and how she's going to do Year 12 exams –
they're delayed and practice ones won't happen
until restrictions are over.

Tuesday is all about Sam
and the subjects she's choosing for next year
when she's in Year 12,
as well as her delayed exams.

By the time it's Wednesday
and it's my turn to sit at the table on mute
and listen to the heads of department
drone on about subject selection
for Year 11, Mum and Dad are
                over it.

              So am I.

I already know my subjects, I tell them.
*English, Specialist Maths, French,
Music Performance, Music Composition.*

Mum rolls her eyes so quickly
it seems like she's the teenager
in this situation.

What happened to Chem and Bio?
she asks, flicking her eyes

from the principal on the screen to me.

Don't need them.
I want to study at the Conservatoire de Paris
after school —
it's based on performance only,
plus speaking French.
I've told you that before.

And how realistic is it,
that you'll get in? Mum asks.
Her question is laced with condescension.

Dad is humming under his breath.

Rani says I'm on track
to achieve a distinction for my exams.
And if I can study music at school with Ms Liu
then I'll have a double chance
to ace the performance.

Darling, Mum tries a different tactic
while the deputy principal
talks about careers of the future.
You are an excellent violinist
but musicians don't make money.
Stick to the sciences —
you could get into Melbourne Uni.
Or do business, like Dad.

Like Dad? I explode into an E minor pitch
so high Mum's ears should fall off.
I don't want to be like Dad
— no offence, Dad —
he stopped playing music.
I want to be like Ettie.

I burst into tears, leave the table.

In my room,
I open the subject selection page
on my laptop
and choose my subjects —
including the two music ones.

CRUX

Welty texts me after dinner.

I'm out the front of yours.

I come out,
see him leaning against our front fence.

What's up?

It's too dark to see him properly
but there's something up.
I saw him in a few online classes today
but he didn't say much.

He takes a while to answer me,
and his voice is cracked when he does.
Your dad still do that big brother thing?

Yeah.

D'you reckon I could talk to him now?
By myself?

It takes me a moment
to get what's going on.

Because even though Finn's place is always
                the best place to hang out,
            it's our garage that has Dad in it.

I'll get him now, I say,
go inside.

Dad's stretched out on the couch,
footy on, cup of tea in his favourite mug,
watching the Bombers play the Roos.

But he gets up straight away,
puts on his beanie and jacket,
goes out to talk to Welty.

Dad comes back in, twenty minutes later.
He'll be alright,
but things are a bit tough.
He'll talk to you when he's ready.
Keep an eye on him, okay?

And I can't tell Dad
that I think he's all shades of cool
because what he does
is beyond a definition of cool
but it's also kind of cringy
when you're the one
who has let him down.

The Bombers won, I offer.

Grace

This time we meet in Ettie's tram,
masks on,
stepping over the council tape
that is meant to keep us out.
As if tape can stop me from being in her tram.

This is so awesome! Crux says, hugging me,
and his black mask shifts against my cheek.

It's actually a family heirloom, this tram.
My grandparents donated it to the park.
And Ettie, her room is right over there,
I point out her nursing home through the trees.
But you can't see it properly now,
there are no lights on
because she's probably having afternoon tea.
I called her when I got here but she didn't answer.

Crux studies the names of the taggers
like an entomologist examines bugs
under a microscope.
They're just tags,
random guys with a texta.
Look at the lettering — amateurs!

So, you up for
breaking the
can't-sit-down-in-a-public-place law? I ask.

Yep, he says, sliding opposite me on a bench.
How'd you get out anyway?
I thought your parentals were tracking
your every move.

They went out together.
I think they're dropping a birthday package
at a friend's house.
Doing a knock and run.
So I'm free to live it up for a bit.

Living it up
by going for a walk with me.
Crux's eyes crinkle
and I can tell he's smiling beneath his mask.

Yeah, you're so distracting.

And then he's looking at me,
                    like really looking,
        and I notice for the first time
                how green his eyes are,
flecked with brown, and he has really long eyelashes,
        and now he pulls his mask down under his chin
                and he leans closer to me
        and I follow his movement
                and pull my mask below my chin
                    and I'm even closer
                and now we're kissing
            and we have forgotten about social distancing.

—

Moments later,
        months later,
            moons later,

I pull away
from the sheer gloriousness
of kissing Crux.

It's almost dark, I have to go.

He kisses me once more,
long and lingering,
standing in the doorway of the tram
where Abby filmed me.
He strokes my hair,
twists it around his fingers
like each strand is as sensitive
as the hairs of my bow.
We're so entwined
it's like we've swapped hearts
and mine is bursting with colour
and his is full of music.

I step down from the tram,
leading him into the park.
Ettie's light is on, see?
I point to her room.

But my arm drops to my side
and I stop walking.

Crux squeezes my hand.
What's up?

My parents.
My parents are standing
in front of the nursing home,
staring at me.
At us.

CRUX

I cycle home –
regret nothing about kissing Grace,
regret everything about her parents seeing us.

Grace

I hold Crux's amethyst closed up in my hand
while Mum and Dad sit down on my bed
while I lean against the wall to
T.A.L.K.

Why is he so obsessed with you, anyway?
            Why didn't you at least let us meet him earlier?
How can we trust you now?
                        You can't see this Crux again.
            We don't understand what's going on with you.

                        No, you don't understand.
            And Crux painted me because I am good.
                        He's not a vandal, he's a guy my
                        age who actually likes me.
            Why would I let him anywhere near you when you're so
            negative about what he does best?

We are at a stalemate
because all the angry words have been hurled
and no-one understands anyone.

Liv barges into my bedroom,
brandishing her phone.

Knock! I shout at her.

Liv, some privacy, please! says Mum.

The news,
Ettie's nursing home is on the news!

We instantly squash around Liv,
and Sam comes running in.

The reporter,
holding a microphone in front of Ettie's nursing home,
tells us there were 177 cases today.
Three deaths from coronavirus.
At the nursing home, one of the carers had the virus
but didn't report it.
Kept turning up to work with a slight cough.

Sam says she's probably on a low wage
and needed the money.
Liv says she needed to put the health
of others before her financial needs.
Dad says he wants to move Ettie out of there.
Mum says Ettie is strong, she'll be okay.

I'm not saying anything
because my parents are stopping me
from doing everything that matters to me
and I can't even see Ettie.

My internal violin plays
the theme from *Schindler's List*
and I'm already in tears a few bars in.

CRUX

I'm scrolling through Insta,
looking at street artists' feeds
when I see Mack has been out and about,
boasting about his paste-ups.
He's almost the only one –
no-one else dares to go out.
Bindy posted that the city is static,
most street art left as it is,
no more conversations happening
between artists.

My head feels red-hot again.

I think of Grace's parents banning her
from seeing me.
        And then I'm not thinking at all.

I grab my bike and a few cans from the garage,
ride out to the city in the dusk.

It's freezing, there's no-one around,
no-one to see me touch up my piece,
lit up by streetlights and the odd car headlights.
Shouldn't take long to cover up Mack's words
and fix art Grace
even if I can't fix the situation with real Grace.

I'm careful,
keep my cans in my backpack,
close to my bike, ready for a quick exit.
I've finished fixing up Grace,
just need to shake my cans for her violin.

A car's headlights illuminate
my piece
    but the lights don't move on.
        The lights stay on, stay still.
           On me.

By the time I've turned around,
ready to grab my bike, get out of here,
there are two police officers
getting out of their car.

—

Hey, kid,
want to explain what you're doing?
one of the officers asks me.
He's tall, with glasses.

I twist the donut on my blue *Atmosphere* can.
In a shaky voice,
I explain the commission,
offer evidence with Fendix's Insta posts
of a paid commission,
show Bindy's photo with Mack's tag
(without mentioning Mack)
– I just wanted to fix my work –
I was not the tagger.

I even show the colours of my cans,
the same colours to match my piece –
not a green or orange in sight.

The police officers confer.
The one with glasses says,
Look, I believe you,
you're not vandalising property

but you're out past curfew,
you're carrying cans that you can't legally buy.
We're going to take you into the station,
your parents can pick you up from there.

He shoves my bike into the rear of their van.
The other one opens up the back door for me.

I am put into a small room,
table, three chairs,
door locked.
No backpack, no phone.

I am left there for fifteen minutes.

I am taken out,
showed a cell,
told the penalties for vandalism,
told my parents are on their way.

I am taken back to the small room.

Then Dad
is brought into the room,
the police officer with glasses watches
as he hugs me.

The officer says,
He's not in any trouble,
but he's out past curfew with spray cans.
Another incident like this
and we're talking community service.

But Dad uses the language
of his brother-to-brother sessions,
to show our stable family,
my squeaky-clean record.

We're allowed to leave.

It's only after Dad and I
have thrown my bike into the boot of the car,
and we're sitting in the front
that Dad reaches out to hold my shoulder
and the hard boulder of anger inside me
toward Mack,
remote learning,
Covid restrictions
and Grace's parents' restrictions
melts and I turn watery, and sniff.

It's okay, says Dad. *You're okay.*

Grace

The aged care home calls Dad.
Ettie is sick.
She has coronavirus.

They'll keep her in the nursing home.
For now.
She would be more distressed
in hospital, they say.
The move wouldn't be good for her.

Dad paces the kitchen.
I should have taken her out,
I should have brought her here.

Mum stops him mid-pace.
Matt, she says gently,
we all have to get tested.
Grace visited Ettie last week.

———

It takes us over two hours,
moving forward
inch by inch in the car,
to get tested.

It takes seven minutes
to answer the nurses' questions,
identify our names, birth dates
and phone numbers,
put up with the swabs up the nose
and down the throat.

The nurse smiles kindly.
Regardless of your results,
you will all need to stay home
in isolation for fourteen days
since you last saw your grandmother.

We are Dalfinches –
it doesn't take us long
to do the maths.

Six days.
We cannot leave the house
for six days.

CRUX

It's raining down so hard and fast
that there is no chance of going out
even if I didn't have to show up for online learning,
even if there was anything to do
in Melbourne's second lockdown.

I stay glued to my phone,
chilled out on my bed,
half an eye on my laptop for Maths class,
deep in multiple conversations,
jumping back and forth.

> Ettie's got Covid.
> We had to get tested.
> Got to isolate.

> Is she ok? Are you ok?

> Not really.

> Are you ok?
> Miss you.

> Same.

And just in case it isn't clear –

> Miss you.

I can't tell her about getting caught by the police.
Maybe she'd agree with her parents –
I don't follow the rules,
I'm a distraction.
Besides, she's got enough going on.

I text Fendix instead.

He flicks a message back.

> Sorry, mate.
> So lucky you didn't get
> community service.
> I can tell you from personal experience
> making wristbands
> for a kids' festival is not fun.

Mum comes into my bedroom,
plugs an oil burner into a power point,
pours in a few drops from small bottles.
Rosemary and basil. To focus.

Mum – I'm kind of busy studying.

That's exactly why you need to focus, Mum says.

When she leaves, I text Fendix back.

> Is the exhibition still on?

> Postponed again.
> Doubt normal life will resume again
> by September.

It's only July.
Still raining, no chance to get out
and I wonder if the rain makes it easier
for Grace in iso.
Type another message.

> Miss you again.

> What the?

> That wasn't for you, Finn!

> Violin girl?

He sends me three red heart emojis
and I let him know
where he can stick them.

> Want to get a burger,
> walk around the block after school?

Can't. Family meeting.
Dad lost his job last week.

> What?

No-one needs marketing.
They wouldn't even let him stay,
so he can't get JobKeeper.
We all have to cut back a bit –
no takeaway etc.
Got to choose between Foxtel and Netflix.

My second family –
and I didn't even know.

Molly sticks her head into my room.
You get oiled, too?
I'm getting a headache,
so many scents wafting around.

Better not tell Mum, I say.
She'll have a crystal or oil
for that, too.

Grace

We've been at home for five days.
Our PCR tests came back negative
but we're still in iso.

No walks. No excursions
to the supermarket, post office, fruit and veg shop.
No takeaway coffees.

The kitchen is too small in the morning.
Whoever makes the first coffee always leaves
the steam wand and milk pitcher dirty.
And we all want coffee at the same time
before the first meeting, first class.

Then we all want the second coffee
at the same time at recess.

We watch Dan the man's presser —
a heart-racing,
mind-boggling,
slumped shoulders
275 cases.

Coles drops off bags of groceries
but they chose the wrong type of pasta
and they didn't include
enough dog food for Griffin.

Mum's flowers are drooping
and she can't go out to buy fresh ones.

Abby comes by after school every day,
takes Griffin for a walk.

I'm only allowed to wave at her
from the verandah.
We shout at each other through our masks.
So frustrating.

Dad calls Ettie's nursing home
three times a day, gets one response.

We all text Ettie — sometimes she texts back.

The sun comes out for a while.
Dad and I bring our laptops
to the outside table
with our headphones.
I practise my French grammar
and Dad uses his professional voice
while drawing expletives
on his notebook
during his meeting.

I scribble a French one,
then translate it in English.

He bursts out laughing
and we both mute ourselves.
Maybe Dad might relent
about Crux
     when Ettie's better.

Hey, Dad, I say,
when he tears off his headphones,
leaves the Zoom room.
I didn't mean what I said the other day,
about not wanting to be like you.
I was just being annoying. Sorry.

Listen to me, Amazin'.
Go all out for your music
BUT have a plan B.
You need a back-up.
Play your violin,
keep studying for your music exams.
BUT keep at least one science.

I smile at Dad, give him a hug.

But I don't know
whether I can compromise my music.

CRUX

We are all at home
sitting outside for a rare moment of sun
when it happens.

One of the kids next door screams,
then there's the sound of broken glass.

This time it's Mum who jumps up,
grabs her phone.

Police, she says.
Domestic violence dispute next door.

The police arrive.
I stare out the front window,
watch two officers get out of their car.

Someone calls an ambulance.
Two paramedics wheel Sasha out,
a towel to her head.
A woman who looks like Sasha
hurries into the house,
leaves with the two boys and their bags.

Alec is taken away in the police car.

Later, an officer knocks on our door,
talks to Mum and Dad.

I stay in my bedroom and wonder if Sasha is okay.

Grace

Iso is finished.

We're free –
to go to the supermarket
and walk within our 5k bubble.
Still can't see Ettie. Still can't see Crux.

———

In Ettie's tram,
lonely as a Melbourne wind,
in the desolate hour of
microwaved dinners
and squabbling children
and too-shiny news presenters
on too-loud screens,
I sit.

Twirl the curled-up leaf I picked up
from the tram's step.

A central stem, strong
brown veins branching to the edges
like roots in soil,
the edges curl in, create
a tiny hollow big enough for a wish.

The leaf fills my palm,
I make the choice not to crush it.

As if another decaying leaf
left to decompose by itself
matters in the scheme of things.

A leaf-life connection.
Mrs Hammond would be proud.
I tuck it inside my violin case.

I can't see anything,
looking in from the outside –
the curtains are closed in Ettie's room.

I undo the clasp of my violin case,
take my violin out,
attach the shoulder rest,
draw out my bow.

All part of the ritual
I've done before Ettie a thousand times.

Only this time with a mask.
Maybe Crux's painting
foretold the future.

I don't even know what to play for her.

It's not like Mozart wrote
'Violin Concerto No. 14'
for sick grandmothers.

I know I'll get stopped.
I have five bars, maybe.

My fingers find the music.
Bach's 'Concerto for Two Violins in D Minor',

that heartbeat of a concerto
that makes you feel less alone
because you need two violinists.

I play the first violinist part for a minute and a half
before a nurse comes running up to me.

I keep playing.
Please, I beg her, in a whisper.
This is for Ettie.

She nods, holds up her palm,
fingers splayed.

Within five minutes,
Bach and I,
my violin and I,
tell Ettie we love her.

—

Five minutes later, I receive a text.

It's not Ettie
but a nurse texting for her.

> Tell that beautiful granddaughter of mine –
> she is a grace note personified.

CRUX

I check on Welty.

> You ok today, mate?

> Today's ok.
> Everything got too much –
> bedroom walls were caving in,
> sucked into screens,
> Mum was working long hours
> trying to keep her business going.
> No footy.

> That sucks.

I try to channel my best Dad impersonation
but I think he'd have other words.

> I didn't even plan
> to talk to your dad –
> I just found myself
> outside your place.

> Want to kick the footy
> before work tomorrow?

> Sure.

Grace

Six days later,
Dan the man is up for his presser,
North Face jacket,
grim determination on his face.

I watch him from my laptop in bed,
still in my pyjamas,
twirling the stem of the crisp brown leaf
I collected from Ettie's tram.

I already know what he's going to say.
He will tell Victorians,

the deflated Victorians,
the number of cases
in the preceding twenty-four hours – 384 –
the number of deaths
in the preceding twenty-four hours
from coronavirus –
six.

It's what he doesn't say that matters, though.

He will not say
– because he will not know –
that one of today's six deaths from coronavirus
is Ettie.

She died alone.
The medical staff around her
would have touched her through full PPE.
Her last sounds would have been the beeps
of medical equipment,
not the triumphant soaring
of Gershwin's 'Rhapsody in Blue',
with those glorious romantic strings in the middle
fading to a gentle whisper of harmony.

There is no more essence of Ettie.

I crush that brown leaf
into fragments so small
their return to earth
will be swift.

CRUX

> I'm so sorry about Ettie.

I don't know what else to say.

> Thank you.
> It's really tough.

> Like darkest stormy blue,
> cyanometer 52?
> Or flat cyanometer zero,
> with barely a hint of blue?
> Or both?

> Yep, both.
> And everything in between.

> Permission to be as ocean stormy
> as you like.

> Thanks.

I send her a blue heart emoji.

Try to stop thinking of the 723 cases today,
and the inevitable deaths that will follow.

Grace

The big wooden doors at the front of the church
are locked.
Hardly fitting for Ettie's funeral.

Dad finds the small side door
and Father George lets us in.

Ettie always liked his sermons –
they were modern and insightful, she said,
and made her think about life
in a different way.

That could be Ettie's tribute right there –
modern, insightful, with new visions for her life.

Dad pats his suit jacket over the pocket,
checks his notes for the eulogy.
There'll be a Shakespeare quote in there, for sure.
I tighten my grip on my violin case.

Ettie is lying in a casket
at the front of the church.
The mahogany colour of the rich honeyed wood
echoes the tone of her violin.

I reach out, stroke the wood,
it's the closest I can get to her.
I imagine it thrumming with her music.

My younger cousins, Charlie and Oscar,
stare at me with their mouths open.

Auntie Laura reaches for Dad,
then steps back.
Dad doesn't. He holds Auntie Laura.

There are only ten of us –
Father George,

Dad, Mum, Liv, Sam and me,
Auntie Laura, Uncle Rob, Charlie and Oscar.

Ettie's brother in Sydney isn't here.
There's no-one from the nursing home.
There are no neighbours, friends, cousins.
The Melbourne Symphony Orchestra
sent a huge flower arrangement
but there should be a whole orchestra
here for Ettie.
She deserves it.

Uncle Rob sets up a video,
Liv sits by the sound system.
Father George puts on his robes.

We sit in our households.
Dad holds Sam's hand on one side,
mine on the other.
I pull my black dress over my knees.

We are quiet, composed, reflective –
on the outside.

We are a torrent of sadness inside.

All my senses are attuned to Ettie.

The coloured lights from the stained-glass windows
dance on the purple carpet.

The solitary leaf from the liquidambar tree
brought in to the altar
by someone's shoe,

red in the middle, bleeding to a faded orange
with torn edges.

Shuffling sounds
as Oscar shifts his three-year-old body
on the hard pew.

Liv's look of concentration
as Dad nods to her when we need music,
and she touches her phone,
connected to a speaker.

Auntie Laura's quietly sniffling
into Uncle Rob's shoulder.
A pungent scent
as Father George walks around Ettie's casket,
swinging and releasing his thurible of incense.

Casket is a better word than coffin –
a treasure within
rather than the end of a body.

Father George says many wise things –
Ettie would approve.

He says, *Even though Covid-19 means*
only ten people can attend a funeral,
that's not such a bad thing.
The support crew for the bereaved
can drop casseroles of condolence at the door.
They don't need to be here
to tell the grandchildren how much they've grown
or to comment on the weather.

Sometimes,
Father George looks at us with a kindly smile

between his greyish-white beard and moustache,
too many mourners can dilute
the sorrow of those left truly bereft.
There needs to be a time to grieve deeply.

Then it's my turn.

Dad gives me a gentle nudge.
I make my way to the altar,
stepping carefully around the lone leaf.

I fix my eyes to the round stained-glass window
at the front of the church
above the closed front doors.

My fingers are comfortable on their strings,
my hand steady on the bow.

I play the opening bars
of Eva Cassidy's 'Autumn Leaves'
then allow my voice
                to be as pure as Ettie's love for us.

I sing of autumn leaves falling
      and reds and golds
            and the approaching winter,
                  which is already here for us
                        and will stay long past
                              the sun returns.

My violin, my voice.
      My violin, my voice.
            My violin, my voice.

No wonder they say the violin
is the closest instrument to the human voice –

it can hold all the feelings,
                    then release them.

When I've finished,
I look over at Dad
because
        Dad
                violin
                        Ettie
                            are all connected.

He's crying.

CRUX

Our 'reflection' piece
must be just that, Mrs Lovind tells us
through Zoom.
Reflective. Thoughtful. Perceptive.

Write a letter to the newspaper.
Begin with one word
to define the pandemic.
Let it flow from there.

> What is this rubbish?

Welty messages us.
I see him rolling his eyes
in his square on my screen.

Forty minutes, Mrs Lovind says.
Start typing now.

Wish I could paint my response instead.
Wish I could talk into Dad's camera instead.

Sigh. Type slowly.

Temporary.
Covid-19 will be a blip in history –
an important one –
a defining one –
but it's temporary.

The yellow crosses on the floor
of the supermarket
to mark social distancing
will start to curl up at the edges,
tear away, stick to the underside
of a trolley-pusher's shoe.
And when eventually
a kid earning $14.10 an hour
is told to scrub the final stickiness clean,
social distancing
will be a term reserved for old memes.

Historians will write about it,
and kids in the future will write essays
about the economic impact
and the pressure on frontline workers
and the added strain of declining mental health.
Those kids
won't experience the closure of schools
but, then again,
maybe remote learning will become normal
in the future
and those kids will wonder
what it's like to be educated face-to-face.

All these people
who are angry, annoyed, frustrated,
anxious, scared –
they don't understand it's temporary.

This too shall pass, and all that,
          not to get too philosophical about it.

Street artist's creed –
the temporary nature of art,
slowly decaying in the sun and rain
or being painted over.

Nothing of beauty lasts forever.
Nothing grim lasts forever.

I think of art Grace,
still on a city wall with Mack's words
sprayed over her violin.
Grace's videos, my posts –
how long will they last online?
How long will this lockdown last?
Will the scars of Covid-19
leave us decaying in beauty or rot?

Grace

I do not play my violin for three whole days.

After the first day,
Dad sits on the end of my bed.
I know it's tough,
I know it's going on forever.
Hang in there, it'll get better.

Play something.
        Anything.

After the second day,
Liv offers to put beachy waves in my hair
with her straightener
even though this winter weather
gives no hint whatsoever
of summer ever returning.
It'll look good over Zoom, Liv says.

After the third day,
Sam makes me cinnamon toast and a hot chocolate
and slides them next to my laptop
in the middle of my French class.
Pour toi, she says.

—

> Checking in.
> What colour today?

> Grey. Flat.
> Can't even play my violin.

> It's ok.
> Even the ocean
> is still sometimes.

—

There are days of G string flatness
after Ettie's funeral.

We eat lasagna three nights in a row.
The one from the school's care group
was too liquid and squishy.

The one from our neighbour
was delicious — cheesy and warming.
I can't even remember what
the third one tasted like.

Mum takes Dad out for long walks —
they come back holding hands.

Liv and Sam bury themselves in VCE study.
They both sneak out
to walk with their boyfriends.

And Mr K emails us —
the musical is cancelled for this year.

Abby is devastated.

> I can't see Ted now.

Meili is disappointed.

> What about the afterparty?

Skylar is dejected.

> I wanted to be part of something fun.

Corona chorus

Saturday, 8 August 2020
Daily Victoria Covid statistics
New cases: 466
Total cases: 14,283
Deaths: 12

VanitaJ
The mental health of all Victorians
is more important
than the relatively few Covid deaths
of the aged.

NotADictator
Open the state, Dan.
Lift our restrictions.

SanjeevP
Reach out if you need help:
Lifeline
Beyond Blue
MensLine Australia
Headspace
Kids Helpline

LoneWolf
I didn't get out of bed today.

AngieW
Thanks for keeping us safe, Dan.

CalliH
Today,
I held my breath until the case numbers came in,
consoled my 12yr old because his camp was cancelled,
avoided someone I knew in the supermarket
because I just couldn't talk to anyone,
remembered my positive affirmations,
forgot my positive affirmations,
made a cake to cheer us up,
watched Netflix, went to bed early.
Tomorrow will be the same.

CRUX

Welty and I stack shelves for masked customers.
Mum's face has almost permanent lines
from her PPE.
The AFL players catch planes with their families,
play footy for us.
We judge the daily numbers
on whether Dan Andrews
is wearing North Face or his suit.
We are over sourdough bread.
The rest of Australia does not care.
Our teachers watch us through their laptops,
checking we don't look off past the screen,
in case we have cheat notes for our tests.
Finn's dad has applied for seven jobs
without getting a second interview.
Welty runs or works out every day –
at least I'm getting fit, he says.
Molly has not met anyone
in her uni course face-to-face.
Grace is so sad
and I can't even give her a hug.
The AUSLAN interpreters for the daily presser
have faces so expressive
they could tell a million stories in seconds.

It's going to be a long winter.

Grace

Someone must have told Abby
I haven't touched my violin.

It's the fourth day after the funeral,
after another day of Zoom classes
that don't matter at all.

Through my window,
I hear the sound of a cello,
a low D chord
that rumbles from the bottom
of the street
upstairs to my window.

Abby has planted herself and her cello
on the footpath in front of my house,
sitting on a small camp stool.
Her mum leans against their car behind her.

Bring your violin down!
She calls up to my open window.

I shake my head.
She starts playing the most staccato version
of a baroque fugue,
the type that makes me jumpy.

Your choice! she sings out,
pulling down her mask temporarily.
It's this or our orchestra piece!

I groan, but grab my violin.

I stand on our front verandah,
start playing a medley of modern string songs.
Abby keeps the base beat with me.
Dad, Mum, Sam and Liv come out to the verandah,
tap their feet.
A few neighbours come out from their houses,
smile, stay awhile.
People walking their dogs past our house
create a small, social-distanced respectful circle
around Abby, and listen to us.

Our last song is 'Golden', Harry Styles.
Playing it for Ettie,
to take us back to the light.

Abby stands up from behind her cello, stretches.
You see, she calls to me. *Restrictions
can't stop our music, can't stop us.*

Later that night, I text Abby.

> Song choice right now?
> Got to be the theme song from Friends.

Aww!

> Lucky for me
> we met in Prep.

Lucky for you
you came down with your violin –
I only know the first few bars
of that baroque piece
but I would have played it
over and over.

Lucky for you
I didn't break your bow!

Lucky for us
we met in Prep.
I miss your Ettie, too.
And it was your mum.
She told me to come over with my cello.

CRUX

It's Molly's nineteenth birthday and, as she can't
be in a pub
(they're shut),
get messily drunk with her new uni friends
(she doesn't have any because
she's only had one day of face-to-face learning),
go to a salon and have a massage or facial
(hardly essential),
she sets up wood and sticks in our outdoor fire pit.

Mum makes her a birthday cake,
Dad puts together a slideshow
of his favourite Molly moments
and I use a fresh canvas to paint her –
wings of fire behind her.

An angel of destruction, Mum says, laughing.
A fairy of light, Dad says sentimentally.
Fire-breathing girl, I say,
and breathe heavily all over her
until Molly swipes me.

We sit around the fire outside
in puffer jackets and beanies,
eating lamb kebabs in our hands.

Before we sing happy birthday,
Mum makes us write down a wish for Molly
on slips of paper, then feed them into the fire.

It's a full moon, Mum says,
pointing up to the dark sky,
perfect for manifesting wishes.

Hmm, I say, pretending to think,
a wish for true lurve
or a wish for 500 more pairs of shoes . . .

Like you can talk about true lurve, Molly scoffs.
I see how often you leave comments on Grace's posts.
I see how she looked at you,
that time she came over.

How did she look at me? I ask it too quickly,
and Molly laughs, doesn't answer me.

We throw our paper into the fire.
Molly lights her own birthday candles.
When she blows them out,
I hope all her wishes come true.

Grace

My feelings toward Mum
are a daisy petal exercise.

I love Mum.
      I love Mum not.

I love Mum.
      I love Mum not.

Mum cooks each of us
our favourite meal, including dessert,
to cheer us up
through the lockdown winter
of our discontent –
even I'm misquoting Shakespeare now.

      I love her.

Then she makes us
go through our wardrobes
to sort out the clothes that no longer fit us.

      I love her not.

She sews us each a make-up bag,
and puts in it an online voucher
for a make-up store.

Golden rose eyeshadow! says Liv.
Ebony waterproof mascara! says Sam.
Kali goddess lipstick! I say.

We kiss Mum, until she flaps us away.

      I love her.

On the report-writing day,
when we have no school,
Mum makes us watch the French news report
so we can listen to a French newsreader
enunciate her words properly.

I have a Maths SAC on Monday, says Liv.
My history essay is due, says Sam.
I've already done an hour of French grammar, I say.

But Mum lines us up on the couch,
turns off the subtitles,
grills us about the latest news stories in France.

I love her not.

CRUX

The family next door are all back.
It's as if nothing ever happened.
Sasha and the kids came back first, then Alec.
Sasha wears a cap low over her forehead
when she ducks out to put rubbish in the bin.

Mum went over to see her
once Alec had left for work.

I overheard Mum telling Dad their conversation.

Sasha eventually agreed to walk with Mum,
her boys a little way ahead.

Cameras.
There are cameras inside their house.

The boys.
One scared, the other angry.

His position.
Who'd believe her over him?

Her family.
They think he's a saint, working so hard,
such a committed doctor, such a good dad,
putting up with her depression.

Depression.
She doesn't have depression!
She has a violent husband.

Bruises.
Her shoulders. Her chest. Her thighs.

Leaving.
If she leaves him, she has nowhere to go.
Her sister can't take her and the boys.

Status.
She only works one day a week.
She lives in a nice house.
She has a shiny car.
She's a doctor's wife. A mother.

Control.
He took away her credit cards.
He checks her phone every day.
She's not allowed to go to the supermarket
or the chemist anymore.

Endurance.
She can cope with the physical abuse.
Not the emotional abuse.
The physical pain fades eventually.
The emotional pain destroys
her sense of herself.

Help.
We've made it worse for her.
He knows we know.
He will not lose face like that again.
He will be more careful

                     how he punishes her.

Maybe Alec needed someone like Dad
when he was younger.

Corona chorus

Sunday, 30 August 2020
Daily Victoria Covid statistics
New cases: 114
Total cases: 19,015
Deaths: 11

Bored
I need a new Netflix series —
suggestions?

PatO
Along with my decluttered rubbish
I've thrown out my busy schedule
my yearly overseas trip
my 12-hour office days
and my marriage.

TimF
If my wife and I can work from home
with seven daily work Zoom meetings
and three primary school kids
in virtual classrooms
then you can too.

KathE
Please,
do not criticise the contact tracers.
They are doing
one of the most important jobs
in Victoria right now.

Grace

Grace! I'm trying to watch the news.
Can you play that thing later?

Mum stands in my bedroom,
takes up all the space, all the air.

I've waited for hours to practise
because everyone had SACs or meetings.

I hold my violin and bow loosely
by my side.

You don't need to practise so much, she says.
It's not as if you're preparing for anything
during Covid.

Mum
— my words are accelerato angry —
I always play my violin,
it's my art, my career.

Mum stiffens.
Grace, you cannot make a career out of the arts.
Focus on science or business or medicine.

I am
    accelerato
        accelerato
            accelerato.

Quickening tempo.

I'm going to focus on my violin.
I don't care what you think.
As soon as I've finished school,

I'm leaving. For Paris.

Mum is
    adagio
        adagio
            adagio.

Slowing down with slumped shoulders
and all the breath and anger oozing out of her.

I want to slam the door
and run,
        run,
            run out into the night.

But it's my bedroom
    and I'm not leaving her in there
        and now she's sitting on my bed
            and we'll have to have a 'conversation'
                and I just want to play my violin.

———

Have you put your VCE choices in?

                         Yep. I've put them in.

And?

                                 English.
                          Specialist Maths.
                              French.
                    Music performance.
                    Music composition.

Music isn't a career.
Mum is yelling at me now

but I am super calm.
Smooth, flat surface on this ocean.

I will change them online myself, she threatens.

> *Students are the only ones who have access*
> *to subject selections.*

I will call the school, regardless.

UNBELIEVABLE.
She is still threatening me.

> *Ms Liu will support me.*
> *Rani will support me.*
> I am about to say
> – Dad will support me –
> when right on cue, Dad walks in,
> he's clearly overheard everything.

Sweetheart, he says to me,
we've been through this.
I know how wonderful you are at violin,
I think you should keep playing in the orchestra,
play in a trio or band if that's what you want.
But so few artists make it –
you need to think of another career.
And really, composition?
It's not like I've heard you writing much music.

> *Ettie made it,* I say,
> frothy waves now inside me.

Ettie was the exception, Dad says.

> *Aren't I exceptional too?*
> Mum and Dad do not answer me.

You need to be able to support yourself,
says Mum.
One day, you might have kids, a mortgage.
You might have a partner or maybe not.

> *Yeah, probably not*
> *since you've banned me*
> *from seeing Crux.*

Mum tightens her lips but continues.
You might have an injury,
and you couldn't play the violin.
Play the violin for pleasure
but choose a career that will support you.

> *Fine,* I mutter,
> worn out, fed up, ambushed.
> *I'll choose the sciences.*

CRUX

No-one is coming or going next door.
Alec's car stays in the driveway.
No-one goes out to the supermarket
or for a walk.

But today,
when I'm cooking up noodles in the kitchen,
I see one of the boys clambering over our fence,
face panicked, arms grasping,
and I run outside
and pull him over to our back yard.

> To safety.

We can't even hear what he's saying
because he's crying so much
but Dad calls the police
and by the time the kid finishes sobbing,
Alec has driven his car off
in a screech of tyres,
and Mum has run next door.

Molly and I sit with the sobbing boy,
Mum brings in his brother,
and we watch Disney movies
on the couch together
while an ambulance takes Sasha to hospital
because she is unconscious.

The boys, Ethan and Liam, are sitting still
on the couch, like stone statues,
Liam with a torn Father's Day card in his hand.

Hey, I say,
*wanna come into the garage,
do some spray painting?*

Their nods aren't very convincing
and they don't speak,
but they follow me to the door of the garage.

I was just about to repaint this wall,
I say, pointing to the smaller brick wall,
the one that faces their house.
It's cyanometer blue 42,
perfect for a powerful owl at night.
But I open it up to the boys.
What d'you you think? What shall we paint on it?

Liam turns to me, and his face is incredulous.
You mean, we can paint anything?
Even a superhero?

Sure, let's paint a superhero, I say.

I don't want him to be like Superman
or Captain America.
I want him to be our superhero,
like he's a superhero only for us, says Ethan.

I've already grabbed a can for the mark-up.
The boys direct me –

Make him bigger!
                    He has to fly with his arms out.
              Like he's flying down to us.
                              He needs to look strong.
                         And have magic powers.
                        He wears purple and green.
       Make him look like he's laughing.

Once I've done the outline,
the boys choose their colours
and the paint flies out of the nozzles so fast,
like they want their superhero
complete and powerful on the wall
yesterday.

When Sasha's sister comes over,
flanked by Mum and Dad and two police officers,
their superhero is almost finished,
with wonky eyes, paint dripping everywhere
and a blank face.

Can you finish him? Soon?
asks Liam, reluctantly passing me his purple can.

Sasha's sister swipes her eyes with a tissue.

Sure! He'll be flying off the wall in no time!

I cast a nervous look at the police officers,
one is looking around the garage,
noting the milk crates of cans,
the canvases stacked up,
the sprayed garage walls.
My stomach is flipping pancakes
and Grace is nowhere in sight.

My son is quite the artist,
Dad has his smooth voice on again.
Studying VCE art, fine arts,
lots of different mediums,
the garage is his studio.

The police officer nods,
focuses back on the boys,
and leads them and their aunt
out the front.

When Mum and Dad come back in,
Molly and I are waiting.
So is this it, now? I ask. *He'll be charged,*
they'll get a divorce?

Mum shakes her head sadly.
This is not a Disney movie.
Maybe he'll apologise, buy her
an expensive gift,
tell her how much he loves her,

she won't press charges
and they'll live together again.
Or maybe he'll be angry,
and it will accelerate.

Molly looks as confused as I feel.
But she's still not safe.
Those boys, they're not safe.

Mum turns to her, fierce.
Molly, of course this is not right.
But it takes enormous courage
to leave the father of your children,
to choose the unknown
over a nice house and your kids' education.
If she leaves him,
she'd have to work more to support the boys,
move house, change schools.
Don't judge her. She's doing the best she can.
It usually takes seven attempts
before a woman leaves her violent partner.
And everyone has a different definition of safety.

I look at my sister. I look at my mum.
I think about Grace.
I think about Sasha, taken to hospital
twice since they moved in.
Seven attempts?

Dad sighs. *The onus is on Sasha to leave,*
while really Alec needs to be held accountable.
But kids will sometimes align themselves
with the parent with power,
just to keep themselves safe.
So, no, it isn't as easy as just leaving.

They'd choose Alec, Molly says slowly,
even after all this?

The world suddenly seems
a lot more complicated than it was before.

Grace

Mum and I are barely talking.

At dinner, I look at Mum's face
while we eat our steak and salad –
same eyes, same hair as me, as Liv, as Sam.

I remember Dad's Shakespeare quote –
'Thou art thy mother's glass,
And she in thee' –
and I shiver.

I do not want to be like her.

I do not know how I feel.
           I do not want to feel what I feel.
       I do not want to look at her.
           I do not want to look like her.
              I do not want to feel sorry for her.
I do not want to think of her never-had-enough-
money-no-security self.
         I do not want want want her to ruin my life.

—

After dinner, I
text
    text
        text
back and forth with Crux,
about Netflix, paint colours, grace notes,
his friends, my friends, amethyst crystals.
And now he has my music heart,
and his colour heart beats inside me,
and the bridge of music and colour between us
is strong and true.

If it were only Mum who banned me
from seeing him, I'd ignore her.
But because it's Dad, too,
I can't add to his sorrow, give him more grief,
when he's almost an old man stooped in half
from Ettie's death.

I just need to wait
        until enough time passes.

CRUX

I look at the wonky superhero,
dripping with splotches and tentative lines.

Got to finish him up for the boys
before they come back from their aunt's place.

I go over Ethan and Liam's lines,
make them stronger, clean up their drips,
paint him a face – laughing.

I think about Mum's words,
about the definition of safety
for Sasha and her boys,
about the definition of graffiti,
how the overwhelming picture of tags and graffiti
might send a message that a place isn't safe.

I don't want to make anyone feel unsafe.
I don't want to add marks to a train station
or someone's work van
so that someone might feel unsafe.

Respect, got to show it to everyone.

I balance on Dad's ladder
with a few cans on the second top step.
I re-spray the superhero's eyes,
add a tiny spray can in the centre —
for this superhero sprays hope.

Grace

After Mum makes it pointedly clear
that I can't play my violin at all today
because she and Dad have back-to-back meetings
and they're too important
for her to be distracted by my noise,
I decide that I've had enough.

Even though my parents made it abundantly clear
that I was never to see
    that boy who painted you,
        that graffitist
            ever again,

I meet Crux for a secret walk.
Abby's my alibi.

Dalfinch daughters always obey
but I no longer care about obeying my parents.
Well, I do care about Dad.
I just hope that his
understanding heart
won't find out.

When Crux sees me, he holds out his arms
and I fall into them.

It sucks, he says, after I've filled him in
on the whole subject selection scenario.

No-one, not even your parents,
should stop you from being you.
You're a violinist,
    you're a grace note,
        you're Grace.
           Crux breathes my name like a flute harmony.

He looks at me, cups my face,
kisses me,
and that bridge of colour and music
between him and me
becomes sturdier and sturdier
until I swear I could cross right over it
into his heart.

                      Because he gets me.

We walk along Bridge Road, and that bridge,
usually full of colour, movement and noise,
is now so quiet.

My favourite place to buy a chai
has closed its doors.
The florist where Dad took us every year
to buy Mother's Day flowers has shut down.
An Indian restaurant has three days of half-price meals
instead of its usual Tuesday night special.

We walk past Jay's bar –
This is where I played,
where Abby first filmed me, I tell Crux.

Jay's sitting in the front of his bar,
working on his laptop.
He sees me, comes out to say hello.

I'll duck back in if anyone comes out,
seeing as nowadays three's still a crowd.

He elbow bumps us both,
asks me about my violin practice.

S'okay, lots of solo practice,
just can't play with anyone except Dad.

He nods, understands.

How's the bar, will you reopen soon? I ask.

As soon as we're allowed, even if it's a small audience.
We'll have to lure them back in,
a lot of people will be scared to come back,
to go out, to mingle. Not quite sure what to do.
I'd love to give the window section a rehaul,
make it look different somehow from the outside.
But there's no money.

He shakes his head to clear it, turns to Crux.
What about you, mate, are you a muso, too?

Crux grins. *Nope, you would not want to hear me
play anything.*

He's a different artist, I say, *a street artist.*

Understanding dawns on Jay's face.
Ah, you're the artist who painted Grace!

The three of us stand in the street
staring, staring, staring at each other
and I think we're thinking the same thoughts.

I whisper my idea, then Jay pulls us around the corner
and we're looking at a plain brick wall
with a downpipe, a small window up high,
a back door to the bar's kitchen.

We do have the same idea.

CRUX

When the four of us sit down to dinner,
sometimes there is nothing to say.
We haven't gone anywhere.
We haven't done anything.
We haven't seen anyone.

But tonight, Mum tells us she stood outside
Sasha's fence and talked with her.

Alec has agreed to go to counselling
on a trial basis.

The cameras inside their house have gone
but he still checks her phone.

The boys can see their superhero
on our garage wall
from the upstairs bathroom window.

Is it any better? Molly asks.

I don't know.

Grace

It's 11.57 pm,
and there are three more minutes
before the Year 11 subject selections close.
For good.

This is what I know —

> If I choose the two music subjects,
> I'll be happy, Mum won't.

>> If I choose the two sciences,
>> Mum will be happy, I won't.

>>> If I choose one science, one music,
>>> Dad will be happy, Mum and I won't be.

My phone is playing quiet music,
the kind that plays in elevators.
I don't want to play elevator music
or orchestra music — all the time.

I want to play music that makes people

DARE

dance *write*

KISS *love*

create

dream

paint

EXPLORE

sing

connect

wake up

All of a sudden,
a song I used to play with Ettie comes on.
She was always up for playing a contemporary song,
and Jason Mraz's 'I'm Yours'
is perfect for strings.

Her last words to me –
She is a grace note personified.

I choose to play the grace note,
add the embellishment. Thanks, Ettie.

I untick Chem and Bio,
add both the music subjects.

Not gonna hesitate. I'm in.

CRUX

I talk to him
when we're riding our bikes,

side by side,
cyanometer blue perfect spring sky.

Dad, I want to change our agreement.
About street art.

Dad turns his head, raises his eyebrows
beneath his helmet,
and his big brother persona flits across his face.
Go on.

I tell him about Jay's bar,
the wall he wants me to paint before he reopens.
It's a commission. I'm by myself.
I try to keep my voice neutral,
but there's an undercurrent of pride
I can't conceal.
Jay will put it in writing.

Okay, but what happens after that?
What will you do when there's no wall to paint next?

Paint in the garage again.

But, Dad asks, pedalling harder up a hill,
> *will that be enough?*

If he expects me
to say yes, he's wrong.

No, it won't,
but as soon as lockdown is over,
I'm going to take my canvases to cafes.
I've finished a dozen birds.
And maybe Fendix
can get his exhibition up and running.

I suck in a big breath of air,
Dad's so much fitter than me
he's barely sweating.
Dad, I swear I won't paint in the streets —
unless it's a commission.

I still don't like it, Dad says.
I don't want you in this world yet.

And there it is —
he wouldn't say that
to any of his troubled teens.
Only to me.
I want to yell at Dad,
but I force myself to stay calm.

Dad, this is my world.
And I've already started —
isn't this a good thing,
that I'm painting
instead of drinking or smoking, doing drugs?

Dad stops pedalling mid-hill,
and it's not because he's tired.
You're right, he says simply.
You're an artist, you're doing it legally,
you're good enough to get commissions.

It's a little awkward to hug Dad
because we're both straddling our bikes
but we lean in.

Thanks, Dad.

Grace

Liv comes home from a weekend bakery shift
with leftovers –
cinnamon scrolls, apple pastries, raspberry tarts.

Mum and Dad are out for a walk
so Liv calls for Sam and me
to come to the kitchen.

Finch princess party! I exclaim
because there has been nothing
to exclaim about lately.

Sam rolls her eyes
but doesn't say anything
because she's already got a mouthful of pastry.

I know she remembers our princess parties –
tablecloth spread on the floor under the table,
one of Mum's flower vases in the middle,
marshmallow teacup biscuits and juice.

Liv bumps her cake into my scroll, Sam's pastry –
Sugar cheers!

I take a deep breath, trust my sugar sisters.
*I'm going to play in Jay's bar again when we open up.
I need you two to cover for me like you did last time.*

Liv shakes her head at me,
older sister style.

What? I say. *Mum's stopping me from doing everything.
Playing in a bar. Choosing music subjects.
Seeing Crux.*

Stop acting like an entitled princess, says Sam.
You're only fifteen.
You're not even supposed to be in bars,
let alone play in them.
And maybe one music subject might be enough.
And Mum hasn't even met Crux,
and you expect she's gonna shower blessings on him
when he painted you all over Melbourne?

Who made you Mum's deputy? I ask,
moving away from the bench, ready to go.
Even the cakes aren't enough
to keep me listening to Sam.

Listen, just concede something,
you'll get something back, Sam says.

But she'll never agree to any of that.

Look, Liv says,
Mum raised us to be strong, independent.
Show her that's who you are.
We never played at being rescued princesses, did we?
You've got this — you can rescue yourself.

I sit down at the bench again
with my sisters,
choose a raspberry tart.

Sam grins. *Liv and I are right, aren't we?*
That's why we rule the kingdom.

I'm still the prettiest, I say.

Corona chorus

Saturday, 12 November 2020
Daily Victoria Covid statistics
New cases: 0
Total cases: 20,345
Deaths: 0

Celebrate
Victoria, we're so close!

SAFriends
We're cheering you on, Vic mates!
Love, SA.

YoungYogaDad
Double donuts!

MostlyMary
Finally, I can see my mum!

DrinkWithDan
Get on the beers!

FamilyForever
Christmas next month is looking good!

HereWeGo!
Top shelf, man!

JaneyS
Here I come, Queensland,
for a summer holiday!

CRUX

I'm three years away from driving a car
and it sucks.
I had to make two bike trips to Jay's bar
with a heavy backpack full of all the cans I need.

Jay borrowed a ladder for me,
it looks a little wonky leaning against the wall.

Good luck, mate, he said,
disappeared inside.

It feels lonely now,
like Fendix and Bindy should
come around the corner
with their crates and ladders.
It's only me,
and the wall seems too large.

But because I know what street artists do
and I'm almost a real street artist
– been paid once –
I snap a photo of that blank wall,
put it on Insta straight away. As Crux.
I'll keep adding to it later
as the wall comes to life.

I stretch out my arms, test the ladder,
shake up a can.
Spray a flat *Midnight Deep*
for the night sky background.

It takes forever,
as there's no scissor lift,

just Jay's ladder,
which I move
          up and across,
                    up and across
                              up and across.

But because I can't quite reach the top,
I decide to let my work just flow up
as high as I can go.

It takes me two hours.
I always have my face to the wall
so no-one can see how old I am
or ask me questions.
Still terrified
the police will come and interrogate me.

Take another quick video,
post it, all the usual hashtags.

The next part, the grid, is the hardest
because I haven't done it by myself.

I take my white *Aspen* can
and start marking up my wall
with random letters.
So far, so good.

Then I snap a photo,
overlay floating Grace from Procreate
on the photo. Grab pink *Flirt*,
start marking up Grace.

I'm all fluid while I can stand on the ground,
hand flowing,

checking, checking, checking my marks,
making tiny adjustments.

But when I have to get up on the ladder,
bend almost sideways,
stretch up to my almost six feet
from the top rung
I lose my fluid lines.
And when I climb down from the ladder
for the third time,
I stand back across from the street
to gain some perspective
and I can see that
                    I'm
                         already
                              out.

I take the green *Field* can,
climb up the ladder, fix up my lines,
move on to the next section.

And now that I'm spraying my outline,
I can see that I haven't quite
got the angle of Grace's hands
around her bow right

        and I'm doubting myself,

                              doubting my ability
                         doubting my art,
              doubting why street art is even worth it,
          doubting why Jay would even want me to paint
                – only because he doesn't have to pay me –
        and doubting how long this piece will even stay
on the wall

because some other artist or tagger
is going to look at it,
see all the amateur lines of it
and paint over it.

Hell, I'd paint over me right now,
and I've barely started.

I drop my phone trying to correct a line,
and when I climb down the ladder again
I see that it's
C R A C K E D
and there are so many cracks on the screen
that I can't see my grid properly anyway.

And I realise, at that moment,
that while I've always wanted
– big –
   – more –
      – scale –
         – to paint large –
I can't do it.

Grace

It feels slightly surreal
for the five of us to be out together.
At Ettie and Jimmy's tram.

We collected the last of Ettie's belongings
from the nursing home,
then wandered across to the park.

Dad has brought
a broom, disinfectant wipes, a candle,
our violins and

                              Ettie's ashes.

Mum sweeps out the leaves and cigarette butts,
Liv and Sam wipe down a few seats.

Dad places Ettie's ashes in their wooden box
on a bench.

Liv lights the candle, holds it,
while Dad and I tune up our violins.

We play Bach's 'Concerto for Two Violins in
D Minor' –
I play the first, of course.

Our music echoes through the tram,
out the open windows and doors,
into the park,
now flush with summer leaves and flowers,
over the road into Ettie's nursing home,
into her empty room.

When we finish, we don't speak
because music takes the place of words

                              sometimes.

CRUX

I start spraying,
    start praying
        that I can make it work.

I've lost time,
and I underestimated how long
it would take getting up and down the ladder,
moving it across the wall.

I've fixed up my mistakes,
work on the outline for the violin now.
I can sense someone behind me
as I climb down the ladder
to move it yet again.

Mack.

The last person I want to see.
I pick up my next can,
spin the donut,
wait to see what he wants.

Saw your Insta posts,
thought I'd check it out, he says.

Yeah? Not much going on here,
just doing the outline.
Nothing to see.
        Nothing to tag.

I'm not here to tag, I'm here to help.
Gotta make it up to you, bro, he says.

I stare at him,
disbelief like an orange drip down a wall
trickling through me.
You wanna help?

Mack gestures to his car behind him.
Got another ladder, got a board.
Save you a lot of time. I'll set you up.

———

By the end of the day,
Mack's outlined Grace's hands,
I've finished the mark-up,
started filling in some colour,
back on schedule.

Thanks to Mack.
He came through for me.

Grace

Well, this is nice, isn't it?
Mum slings her arm around me
as we walk along the streets of Richmond.

She doesn't know
that where I'm taking her won't be so nice.
At least to her.

It's warm enough not to need a hoodie,
even though it's almost dusk.
She should still be able to see,
to see me.

Good to see some of the shops almost ready to open.
See, that homewares shop has changed its window?

Mum, I reckon you have enough knick-knacks.

Always room for one more, Gracie!

We're almost there,
so I slow down
because . . . because . . . because . . .

The definition of a Dalfinch daughter
has to change.
I am more than my parents' expectations.
I am my own possibilities, my own dreams,
and I'm going to be the one
to make them happen.
Rescue myself.

This way, Mum, around here.

I lead her around the corner of Jay's bar,
point to Crux's piece.

I. Don't. Say. Anything.

She stares and stares,
walks the length of the piece,
touches it gingerly as if it might still be wet.
Crosses the road to see it properly
from a distance.

I follow her and we lean against a wall,
looking at floating Grace
against a star-studded midnight blue sky
like the Chagall painting
Crux showed me.

So, I say,
these are all the things I've done wrong.

She stares at me, impassive.

One, I've been seeing Crux.
I like him, I like him a lot.
And, he painted me. With my permission.

Two, I changed my subjects back.
I'm down for both music subjects next year.

And three, I'm playing with Rani and Jay here
tomorrow night.

Mum's face is still, her arms are folded.

But this is what I'm doing right.
One, I'm telling you everything now.

Two, I've already got my exam results back.
Straight A's – for all of them.

Three, I'm following your lead.
No plan B.
I will not fail at music, I promise you that.

Four, I emailed the careers counsellor –
I'm going to swap Music composition
for Biology.
I'm not really a composer, and I like science.

Five, I want to invite Crux around for dinner.
So you can meet him properly.

She finally speaks.
Is this what you really want?

I nod.

Your choice, Grace.
But you drop one per cent off an A
and I won't pay for a single music lesson.

I nod. This is going better than I think.
She hasn't tried to stop me.
And will you come and hear me play?

She shakes her head,
and she looks as if she has given up on me,
as if I am beyond her care.

It's what I've always wanted,
to be beyond her micromanaging,
but now it doesn't seem
as if that's what I want at all.

She walks away
       without me.

CRUX

There's enough sun to throw a glint
of hope on floating Grace.

The wall is everything I hoped it would be –
an overscale Grace with her violin
floating in a cyanometer blue 31 sky,
smiling to herself.

Bindy, Fendix and Issa turn up,
admire the art.

There are fifty people allowed inside.
Hands sanitised, QR codes activated.

Dad, Mum and Molly stand in front of my piece,
then say hello to Grace.

Mum puts her hand in her pocket,
sneaks a look at me,
then slips something into Grace's hand.
Grace smiles.

It's an opalite, for communication, Mum whispers to me
when she's close enough.
Not that she needs it,
that girl plays the songs of the angels.

Fendix talks to Dad,
gestures toward the wall, with my signed name, Crux.

Mate, says Dad, walking over to me,
clapping me on the shoulders,
you've done something extraordinary.
You were right – this is your world.
Lucky Melbourne.

I've just figured out Dad's tatt –
a huge X inside a heart
to show Dad's ability
to get to the crux of the matter,
straight to the core.

Finn and Welty show up.
Get around him, lads, this is huge, says Finn.

Welty nudges me,
nods to where Grace is talking to her friends.
Hey, take us over to your violin girl's friends.

Grace gestures to me with her bow.
We're about to start, Rani and Jay are ready.

I find a seat inside, listen to Grace play.

Grace

I will never forget tonight.
Even though I've played here twice before,
this time it was different.

I wore my black tube skirt
and pink handkerchief of a top from Italy,
and I played,
not because I'm a Dalfinch daughter
and we do everything well.

                                        I played because
                                          this is me.

I might not have Ettie to play for anymore,
but I have Crux.

And Dad and my sisters.
And Mum.
Mum is here to listen to me play.
I almost missed her
because – like me –
she's short and hard to spot in a crowd.
But she's here.

———

After everyone has left the bar,
Crux pulls me aside.

He holds a box out to me.
I made you something.

Inside the box is a wooden ring
marked in fifty-two equal pieces,
each one painted a different shade of blue
ranging from the lightest white blue
to a strong grey.

On each colour he's written an emotion –
from stormy, fierce, angry,
to calm, accepting, balanced,
and exhilarated, empowered, loved, seen.

A cyanometer,
I gasp. *But this . . .*

It's your ocean of emotion,
Crux says,
So you know you're still on the ring.
No matter how many colours you feel in a day
or even in a moment.
You are the drop and the ocean.

I hold it up to the sky,
still blue this early into the night.
There's a vivid blue behind the bar,
a serene blue behind a cloud
and a whiteness to the east.
I spin around.

So I'm serene, glorious and unsettled all at once.
I laugh. *Truly all the ocean views!*

I point to the most vivid, purest blue
in Crux's cyanometer.

I blush.
This is how I feel right now.

And I kiss him.
The sky blushes too.

Acknowledgements

It's taken me over a decade of committed writing before this debut book made it out into the world. I'm so grateful to my village.

Thank you to Danielle Binks for giving me a chance, for guiding me through publishing contracts, for being a strong advocate for young adult literature and just . . . everything. You are a multicoloured street art mural and whole symphony combined.

I would need every shade in a cyanometer and every note on a violin to thank the Hachette team! Kate Stevens – your passion for Grace and Crux's story has carried both *Grace Notes* and me. Thank you for your constant reassurance, your high publishing standards and for our creative brainstorming conversations. Stacey Clair, editor extraordinaire – thanks for your detailed work on *all* the things. Vanessa Pellatt – your attention to detail and insightful questions helped me become a better writer. Simon Paterson and Samantha Collins at Bookhouse – thanks for setting my words beautifully on the page. Rebecca Hamilton – thank you for your detailed proofreading. The wonderful sales, marketing and publicity teams – thank you for your passion and energy.

Karen Farmer – thank you for bringing Grace to life with your stunning stencil art; her beautiful face, that textured background! Astred Hicks – thank you for creating a magnificent cover for Grace and Crux's story.

Lukas Kasper – thanks for letting me hang around with you, ask many questions and for checking that my street art world sounded legit.

Nathania Camargo and Blakely McLean-Davies – thanks for putting up with the screeching sounds from my violin and for checking that my violin lingo rang true.

Nova Weetman, Lorraine Marwood and Nicole Hayes – thank you for your support and kind words.

Renee Mihulka – your combined honesty, encouragement and writing talent make you the perfect critique partner and friend. I am so lucky we met when we did!

Lee, Kristine, Marty, Ness, Dave, Leane, Justin, Eleanor, Angeline, Marnie, Kathryn, Natasha – your friendship makes life meaningful.

My bookclub – thank you for our lively discussions over cheese and wine and for your encouragement and friendship. And especially to Rachel for guiding me with the domestic violence scenes and to Kate for advising me on the life of nurses during 2020.

The Springfield Wild Writers – your support has been integral to this book and your friendship integral to me. Special thanks to Kinchem Hegedus, who is equal parts generosity, inspiration and intuition.

Kate Forsyth – your encouragement, creative conversations and your knack for asking the right questions has inspired me in so many ways.

Mum and Dad – how can I express in a few words my thanks for a lifetime of being surrounded by books?

Thank you for fostering my love of literature from the very beginning, reading my school essays and for always supporting me. Literary discussions with Mum, an editing inheritance from Dad; the perfect upbringing for a writer and editor. Claire, Nico, Paul, Chris and Kirrilly – thanks for sharing books, holidays, Sunday night dinners, family memories; your support means everything.

And finally, Brett – thank you for putting up with my oceans of emotion and for always believing in me. You sent me a bunch of flowers early on in our dating days when I started a new novel. I never finished that story but thank goodness ours is still going. Tom, Annalise and Joe – your thoughtfulness, humour, conversations, creativity and the varied ways you make your own paths in the world are always inspiring to me.

—

Karen Comer is a freelance editor and presents writing workshops to children and adults. Earlier in her career, she worked in educational publishing and was the editor for children's art magazine *BIG*. She lives in Melbourne. *Grace Notes* is her debut novel.